SEDUCING THE STRIPPER

LINDSAY EVANS

Red Hills Publishing

Chapter 1

The last thing Tess wanted to do was be at a strip club on a Saturday night, but here she was. But at least she was doing it for love. She led her best friend, Maya, and the two other women into Club Bang-Cock, a strip club with the hottest hung studs in Atlanta. Or at least that's what the flyer said. Normally Tess would be all about "hot and hung studs," especially since this outing had been her idea as part of Maya's bachelorette party. But she'd been unexpectedly called into work earlier that afternoon to resolve a bullshit situation and now was well on her way to a shitty mood.

"Damn! This place is hot!" One of the other women, Lisa, shimmied to the music as the hostess showed them to their table.

Tam, who Maya and Tess had also known since high school and who was visiting from Miami for the wedding, watched everything with a very pleased smile. Dressed in a bright yellow, full-body unitard that showed off her buttery brown skin and thin but curvaceous body, she attracted her fair share of admiring glances.

"These guys are hot!" Maya said, looking around the club at the bow-tied waiters and disco balls glittering above their heads. Already halfway drunk and with her "bride-to-be" tiara on, she was ready to party. "How did you all even find this place?"

"Groupon, girl!" Lisa said with a laugh, tossing her long hair along the bare line of her shoulders.

She was the Groupon queen. Half the new shit she got into—in-door rock climbing, hot yoga, full body waxes—was because she'd seen them on Groupon and was willing to try them at a bargain. Lisa was the wild one among them.

Tess smiled her thanks as the hostess sat them near the stage and slid menus in front of them with a friendly smile of her own.

"Alex will be the one taking care of you ladies tonight." The hostess smiled again. "Have a great time tonight." Then she left them to start that good time.

Tess looked around. Club Bang-Cock was loud, and big. At 8 o' clock on a Saturday night, the place was filled wall to wall with women and a few stray men. The alcohol looked plentiful, the laughter loud, and hand-some men wove through the crowded room carrying trays and ready to serve anyone who asked.

They'd been shown to their table during a break in the show. The stage lights were bright and the muscular MC on-stage, bare-chested and wearing leather pants that looked like they'd been poured on, was saying something about the upcoming act.

If the dancers looked anything like him, Tess knew Maya would be happy to watch them all night even if they couldn't dance worth a damn. She exchanged a smile with Maya and her best friend giggled, adjusting the tiara on top of her short coils.

"This was the best idea!" she said.

"What can I get you ladies for the evening?" A man appeared at their table with a small notepad already in hand.

The table took a collective gulp of breath. Their waiter was mouthwatering, smiling big enough that between his body, surprisingly elegant in black slacks and a white button-up shirt, and his perfectly white teeth, he was already guaranteed a big tip. And he was tall, standing over their table in a way that made Tess feel sheltered instead of loomed over. A strange enough feeling to get from a stranger.

Lisa leaned forward first. "Anything you got, I'll take." She grinned at him, flashing her cleavage and her own brilliant smile.

That usually guaranteed her at least a second look, but their waiter, probably used to women and men throwing themselves at him before even knowing his name, only smiled back in practiced flirtation and flipped open his notepad.

"The Raging Orgasm is our special of the night," he said with a wink he distributed evenly around the table.

The entire table laughed. Even Tess, the group cynic, had to smile at that. He was doing his job very well.

Without even asking him what was in the drink, Lisa said, "We'll all have one."

"Perfect. Four raging orgasms coming up." Then he was gone.

Tam, more practical than Lisa, made a noise of dismay. "You don't even know how much those drinks cost!" She was an artist, not exactly a starving one but still, she kept a sharp eye on her money.

"Don't worry about it, honey," Lisa said. "It's taken care of."

She and Tess had already talked beforehand about costs for the bachelorette party and how to make sure Maya had a good time. The price of a Raging Orgasm was nowhere on the list of things they needed to worry about.

"Ladies!" On stage, the MC was introducing the next act. "Fresh from your fantasies, throw your panties in the air for Black Magic Johnson!"

If there was ever a time to use the term, "the crowd went wild," this was it. All around the club and closest to the stage, the women rose to their feet to cheer and shout, a thunderstorm of sound that followed the retreat of the MC from the stage then rising impossibly louder to a full roar when *Often* by The Weeknd started to play.

"Oooh." Lisa sat up in her chair, her eyes trained on the stage. "This is going to be good."

Tess barely paid attention when their waiter—Alex was his name, she vaguely reminded herself—came by with their drinks and disappeared again. She'd seen *Magic Mike* and *Chocolate City* in preparation for their night out but was still surprised when the spotlight seemed to explode on the stage and show a shirtless man in black. Muscled. Glistening. Dark jeans low enough on his hips to show off that hot triangle of muscle at his hips. The size of his dick was impressive under the denim. And his dance moves, fluid and aggressive that went perfectly with the bass-heavy song, made it seem like he was mentally fucking every woman in the room.

At the end of it, Tess was more than a little

impressed. So impressed that her sour mood was disappearing as fast as the Raging Orgasms in their glasses.

"Damn!" Maya fanned herself with the spread of dollar bills Lisa had given her.

Her bare shoulders glowing with sweat, Tam leaned toward the stage with a dazed look. Apparently, they'd both been too stunned by Black Magic Johnson to run up to the stage with the money they'd gotten out to tip the dancers.

"Totally worth it, right?" Tess asked with a laugh. The night was getting better by the minute.

"Hell, yes!" Maya giggled and raised the rest of her Raging Orgasm high. "To the best bridesmaids and maid of honor a girl could ask for."

Tessa was finally beginning to relax. She raised her own glass. Then almost dropped it. The Raging Orgasm was heavy as hell. In a glass about as big as Tess's head, rainbow colored, and decorated with damn near half a pineapple, the drink was sweet enough to make her open her mouth again for another sip. But it wasn't strong enough to mean their only drink of the night.

Their waiter definitely knew what he was doing. He came back again when the MC was doing his thing on stage, spreading around an effective blend of professional flirtation and masculine solicitousness Tess had never experienced before.

"We're great, gorgeous," Lisa assured him after he'd brought the round of appetizers and shots she ordered for everyone.

"Good." He winked at the table at large. "I'll be gone for a few minutes but will be right back in about ten minutes. If you need anything, Trevor—" he gestured toward the waiter serving a nearby table. "—will get you anything you need."

"We'll wait all night for only you," Lisa said with a cooing smile, making Tessa roll her eyes.

She loved her friend but sometimes she was too damn much. The poor boy must feel like he was on the menu too. And he was a boy, Tess thought, barely legal. And she was being generous because you had to be at least twenty-one to serve alcoholic drinks.

When he left to go tend to whatever it was he had to do, Tess poked Lisa. "Stop making that boy feel like a piece of meat."

"Did you notice where he works?" Lisa curved a mocking eyebrow at Tess. "This is Club Bang-Cock, honey." The way she emphasized "cock" was especially dirty.

"Chill, y'all." Maya drank another mouth full of her Raging Orgasm and pointedly turned her chair toward the stage. But she was smiling. "I'm sure there's enough of him to go around."

Tam laughed. Tess and Lisa's disagreements were always funnier to those around them, no matter how big or small. And that was because, at the heart of it, the two women were so alike that they often rubbed each other raw.

If, like Lisa, Tess didn't have anyone to take care of and made more than her middle management salary, she'd probably live in a downtown condo and travel all the time too. As it was, she had a very different life. A different set of responsibilities.

Even as Tess thought it, she knew it wasn't true. She was too much of a coward to leave Georgia or her sister for something different, something that could be better than the stifling sameness of the town where she was born. Even when Maya had suggested a place they could go together time and time again. She didn't want to leave her sister, she was scared Tracy wouldn't survive without her.

"Ladies, you've waited long enough!" The MC boomed from the stage. "One of our newest and most popular dancers." He paused, one hand near his hip, fingers spread near the thick shape of his dick in the leather pants. "Are you ready?!" The noise of the crowd rose to a nearly deafening level, and he laughed, jolly as a centerfold Santa Claus. "Since you *are* ready, welcome to the stage…Jack Hammer!"

The house lights abruptly dimmed. Then flared to life again, just as Ludacris' *What's Your Fantasy* started to play.

"Oh my God!" Lisa jumped from her chair, her teeth flashing in a wide grin. "It's our waiter!"

Tess turned from smiling at Lisa's infectious enthusiasm, and damn near swallowed her tongue. On the stage, the flirtatious but professional boy who'd been serving them Raging Orgasms all night moved like a snake in the brilliant spotlight. Tess blinked at the sight of his tight and toned body, oiled to show off his defined pecs and rock hard abs. Blue jeans and high top sneakers completed the outfit that was giving Lisa fits. Letting loose a loud wolf whistle, Lisa ran up to the stage with a wad of dollar bills clenched in a waving fist.

With the hard driving beat, the boy was moving his hips in fluid strokes that dried Tess' mouth. At the same time, she wiped the corner of her mouth, convinced she was drooling. On stage, his sweet and gorgeous face was all shadowed planes and angles, the lights making him look both older and more mysterious than when he was serving them drinks and flirting with them like crazy.

"I think I'm about to pass out." Maya clenched her fist around the stack of dollar bills. "That boy is *fire*…"

Maya wasn't joking. Tess was feeling a little bit of the heat herself, her earlier bad mood officially gone.

"Go up there and put that money in his G-string." Tam nudged Maya with a naughty smile. "Damn! If you don't, I will."

Alex dropped down to the floor of the stage and began doing what might as well be sex push-ups. His muscular arms straining as he pushed himself up off the hard floor and rolled back down with his hips. Hips that worked sinuously as if he had a woman beneath him. He looked up with each hip thrust, meeting the gaze of every woman staring at him, his body moving sinuously to the fast and dirty song.

A flurry of bills rained on the stage all around Alex and just didn't stop. He rose to his feet and ripped away the jeans.

The crowd screamed, and Tess damn near lost her breath. The black G-string barely covered him.

Maya shrieked and grabbed Tam, dragging her up to the stage where Lisa was throwing all her money at Alex. From where she was sitting, Tess saw Lisa yelling something in Maya's ear, probably encouraging her to climb up on stage and molest the boy. But Maya only laughed like a loon and threw her money at Alex as he rolled his hips at the crowd a few feet away, the snake barely contained in his G-string threatening to hypnotize them all.

Maya, Lisa, and Tam were still standing at the edge of the stage when the last thumping beats of the song faded away. Tess felt stuck to her chair. The tops of her thighs felt wet and sticky, proof that she was just as affected as the rest of the women in the club.

Oh. My. God.

"Give it up for Jack Hammer!" The MC stood back while a slim-hipped young man walked across the stage with a bucket, collecting all the money on stage. "If you want to see Jack Hammer come up here again, make some noise."

The tide of mostly feminine voices rose up, deafening and certain. "Jack!" They chanted. "Hammer!" And over and over again until they sounded like a mob threatening to grab Alex from wherever he had disappeared off to and force him to strip for them again.

The MC's laughter rolled through the large room. "Since you all ask so nicely, I'm sure we can arrange something for you later on tonight."

But Tess was pretty sure Alex wasn't coming back to the stage any time soon. He had a few tables of thirsty women to serve.

Lisa dropped down into her chair with a breathless laugh, eyes flickering around the room, most likely looking for Alex. All the cash she'd taken up to the stage with her was gone. "Damn, if I'd known what was under that waiter's uniform, I'd have tried harder to get into his pants."

"You are *not* ditching us to score with some random stripper you just met, Lisa." Tam cut her eyes at their friend.

Lisa grinned. "There's always tomorrow."

"Leave that boy alone," Tess said with a shake of her head, although she wasn't one to talk.

"Don't pretend you wouldn't jump him too!" Lisa

threw a wadded up napkin at Tess, and the other women laughed.

By the time Alex came back, they'd all finished their Raging Orgasms and were ready for more. He appeared at their table with his notebook, once again wearing the white button-up shirt, black bow-tie, and black slacks. Although his performance was a good twenty minutes before, he was slightly breathless and a gleam of baby oil showed above the collar of his shirt.

Lisa pounced right away. "Alex, you've been keeping secrets from us."

"Secrets keep a relationship interesting." He flashed his flirtatious smile at them. "Another round of drinks, ladies?"

Tess watched him in admiration—definitely not sexual interest. He was giving them no more or no less than they paid for: attention but nothing focused too long on just one woman. Professional. Personal. Efficient. How did he manage it with so many women begging for his attention all night? A piece of paper flashed in her peripheral vision and she dropped her eyes to the table just in time to catch Lisa slipping him her phone number.

Tess was not jealous. Absolutely not.

She looked away from their exchange when her phone vibrated in her purse. Who was trying to call her right now? Everyone knew she was at Maya's bachelorette party and wouldn't be free until Sunday morning. After a few seconds, the buzz in her purse died down, only to start again. She frowned. Was it an emergency? She reached into her bag. Her sister's face glowed from the screen of her cell. A spike of worry pulled her out of her chair and she tapped Maya on the arm.

"I'll be right back," she told Maya.

"Everything cool?"

"I don't know…family stuff maybe." She accepted the call and put it to her ear, already making her way through the crowd and to the front door of the club.

"What's going on, Tracy?" She raised her voice above the noise.

"Thank God I reached you!" Her younger sister just about shouted at her through the phone.

Tess tightened her grip on the cell phone as she made her way out the door, showing the club's plastic bracelet on her wrist to the host then the bouncer with a vague smile. Despite the lateness of the hour, a decent sized crowd was still in line waiting to get in, their excited voices threaded with laughter and the sound of the hard-driving music pouring from inside the club. Tess passed the long line of women and turned the corner to find someplace a little quieter. She ended up at the side of the building between the club's painted brick wall and a high wooden fence. Metal patio furniture, two round tables and eight chairs in a random configuration, slumped under the low lights glowing from the low roof of the building. Tess didn't bother to sit down.

"Everton just walked out with all my money," Tracy said. "I need some until next week."

But Tracy didn't need Tess' money. They both knew it. At this point in their lives, with Tess being thirty-four and Tracy twenty-four, these cries for help were more habit than anything else. After their parents died nearly eight years before, Tracy became used to relying on Tess and Tess got used to being relied on. Now though, Tracy had a decent job and could pay the mortgage Tess helped her to get as well as keep supporting the never-ending string of bums who came into her life and her bed. But Tracy was from the school of "why spend mine when I can spend yours," even when it came to Tess.

"This couldn't wait until tomorrow?" Tess gritted her teeth.

"I want to catch you before you spend it all. I know it's Maya's bachelorette party."

Tess stared at the phone in shock. "You don't get to tell me what to do with my own money, Tracy," she said when she could find her voice again.

"That's not what I mean."

But it was. Tess felt the old anger building up. The same one that made her resentful of her little sister who never had to take care of anything in her life and who just transferred her problems to Tess after their parents died. She felt like screaming, but quietly hung up instead.

One day she had to stop this dance with her sister. *One day.*

The tendrils of responsibility for her sister had been growing stronger and more intrusive, choking off her life since their parents died. In the semi-dark alley, she felt those tendrils tighten even more. They strangled a shout out of her. The sound ricocheted off the dark brick, echoing in the alley thick with the smell of old smoke, stagnant water, and the faint bitterness of past complaints. Pain slammed into Tess' hand and she abruptly realized she'd smacked the wall hard, a sting vibrating into her hand and up her arm to settle like an aborted war cry in her chest.

But this wasn't something she did. Hitting inanimate objects out of frustration. Except, of course, when she did. Tess drew in a deep breath and straightened, tugged down the hem of her blouse and wiped all traces of emotion from her face.

"Don't do that." A shape uncoiled from the shadows closest to the building and she jumped. "Don't put on that mask." The low voice rumbled over her, and a man stepped fully from the shadows.

"Alex?"

He walked closer to her, looking even taller than when he'd served her and her friends at the table. "My name is actually Elijah," he said.

So close to her, he was a solemn figure in the black and white. Not the super-sexy "Jack Hammer" and not even flirtatious Alex. Simply undeniably attractive and male. The planes of his square-jawed and full-lipped face were even more distractingly handsome away from the chaos of the club.

"You shouldn't have to pretend to be something you're not," he continued. "Not out here by yourself, or with your friends."

"You mean I shouldn't have to pretend like you do?" Her surprised embarrassment put the rude words on her tongue.

"That's part of my job," he said with a flash of Alex's grin. Then the grin fell away, leaving his face in somber lines once again. "The mask you put on doesn't make the pain inside any easier to bear. Sometimes, it makes things more difficult."

Tess frowned and backed away even as his words struck a chord inside her. She was used to being the one in charge, being the one everyone turned to, even the men she slept with. Living up to everyone's expectations was exhausting, especially at times when she wanted to just rest her head on the nearest surface and close her eyes. But this man, Elijah or Alex or whoever was a stranger. She had no reason to listen to him and no reason to trust what he said.

Tess drew another breath and straightened lapels of her blazer, preparing to dismiss him.

"Don't you have to go back to?"

A brief look of amusement touched his face. "I had to take a break."

"A smoke break?" With his ridiculously fit body, he didn't seem the type to smoke.

"A reality break." He tossed a gaze toward the club with a quirk of his lips. "We all need them every once in a while."

Tess noticed now the tension in his shoulders and the rigid line of his back. Like he was dealing with some pain and turmoil of his own. She had the urge, sudden and strong, to ask him what was wrong, to touch the hard line of his back in comfort.

The noise from the club seemed suddenly far away, swept aside by the strange intimacy that had sprung between them in the alley smelling of smoke and desperation, and a little like sex.

Tess jerked with awareness. She was in a dark alley with a strange man. Alone. Charming or not. Attractive or not. She didn't want to give him the wrong idea, especially her friends had basically been propositioning him all night.

"Listen, thanks for your…whatever." She took toward the front entrance. "I'll see you inside."

Elijah settled a thoughtful look on her. "I hope you find a solution to whatever's troubling you." He made a vague gesture to the phone she still held in her hand.

Tess gave him an unsteady nod and got out of there

as fast as she could with her dignity intact. When she made it back inside to the table, the party had continued on without her. Maya, Lisa, and Tam were all dancing near the stage while a nearly naked man, chest hair and happy trail included, did a bump and grind within inches of their faces.

Relieved she hadn't ruined their good time by taking her sister's call, Tess tossed back half her drink, wincing when the chunk of pineapple in the glass rolled down and bumped her nose.

She put the glass down and was about to join her friends when a hand touched her elbow.

"Can I get you anything else?" Elijah…Alex was back at work.

Concern tipped the corners of his mouth, but there was something else there too. Tess spent too long trying to figure out what it was instead of answering his question. She shook her head when whatever it was still eluded her.

"Pineapple juice?"

"You got it." Then he was gone. Back to being efficient Alex.

The girls came back to the table just as the pineapple juice arrived. Maya dropped into her chair with a breathless laugh while Lisa and Tam tossed a pile of dollar bills in the middle of the table.

"This is money well spent," Lisa said with a giggle and Tam answering laugh said she more than agreed with her.

"Everything cool, Tess?" Maya despite the drunkest of them all, spared her a worried look. She slid a hand across the table, the more tactile of the two of them, and squeezed Tess' limp hand.

Tess tried for an unconcerned smile. "Yes. Completely. That was just Tracy on the phone. You know how that goes."

As if they'd rehearsed it, her three friends rolled their eyes.

"That girl needs to stop calling on you when things get even a little tough," Tam muttered.

"Fixing all her problems only adds more problems for you, Tess," Lisa added her part. "If there was an award for shittiest sister of the year, Tracy would win it every time."

Maya was only sober enough to add: "Amen!"

"Let's not talk about Tracy. Everything is good, I told you. We're here to have fun and celebrate Maya and that's what we're going to do." Tess raised her glass of pineapple juice that Alex had fixed to look like a cocktail. "Right?"

Lisa didn't hesitate. "Right!" She grabbed her own drink, frowned when she saw it was nearly empty. Before she could open her mouth to complain, Alex was there with another round of drinks.

"Ladies." He served his killer grin along with the drinks all around the table, prompting even Tam, who never had to try and attract any man, to make sex eyes at him. "Do you ladies need anything else?" he asked.

"Only you for the rest of my life." Lisa blew him a kiss then started laughing halfway through it.

Alex only smiled and winked. "I'm not sure you could handle me."

Lisa growled and half draped herself across the table, nearly upsetting all their drinks. "Challenge accepted!"

He left before any of them could see what her accepting his so called challenge looked like.

"That boy is sex on two legs." Lisa sighed after taking a long swallow of her drink. "The things I could make him do…"

"I think he's just doing his job, Lisa," Tam said, although she gave Alex's disappearing figure a heated glance. She had some sort of sugar daddy arrangement down in Miami but everyone knew she was just biding her time with him until something better came along. Or until she got bored.

"I wonder if I can make Max dress up every once in a while," Maya wondered out loud about her construction worker fiancé. "Our waiter makes those slacks look good." Maya drew out the last word like she was tasting it on her tongue.

"Our waiter's name is Alex," Tess said, smiling through her censure, but her best friend wasn't having it.

"We are at a *strip club*, Tess," Maya said. "Lighten up. The boy knows he's nothing but eye candy to us. There's no need for any of us to remember his name."

Which was probably why he gave them a fake one, Tess thought.

"Fine. I know you love your anonymous boy toys," Tess said, although Maya was as monogamous and relationship-oriented as they came.

It was the right thing to say because Maya grinned again and tossed the smooth length of her hair over one shoulder. She grabbed some dollar bills from the table. "You know I do," she said, shimmying to her feet and heading toward the stage where another act was about to start.

Tess made a show of rifling through her bag in

search of singles while urging the other girls to join Maya. But she knew exactly where she'd put her dollar bills. She just needed time to breathe.

With each passing second, she was getting more tense, but she needed to relax so Maya could have a good time. This wasn't about Tess and her family's bullshit, this wasn't even about her hurt feelings and the fact that she still couldn't believe Maya was leaving Atlanta without her after all these years. It wasn't that at all.

A few tables away, Alex was giving some other women what they'd paid for with the cover charge to get into the club. Charming and helpful, guessing what they wanted before they voiced it, keeping out of the way of their grabby hands while still sweet-talking them into spending more money. He must have sensed her looking at him because he looked up then, the dark oasis of his eyes easily capturing Tess's gaze and making her swallow hard. She remembered the intimacy between them in the alley, the unsmiling certainty of him that was impressive given his age. She squirmed under the press of her sudden and unwanted attraction, pressing her thighs together under the table when his gaze dipped down. She didn't know whether it was to her mouth or her breasts. Either one was ridiculous.

Tess looked away, grabbed her dollar bills and practically ran to the edge of the stage where Maya and the girls were enjoying an eyeful of the stripper's gyrating dick. She joined them, emptying her mind of everything but the manic feeling that this was one of the last few times she'd get to see Maya. That thought obliterated everything else.

Five acts and nearly a hundred dollars later, Maya and the other girls were done. Giggling like teenagers, most of their tip money gone, they were white girl wasted and hitting on Alex to the point of sexual harassment. That was Tess's cue to get them out of the club and back home.

An Uber took them home to Maya's relatively big house in Grant Park and Tess wrangled them into the king-sized bed in the guest room reserved for when they all slept over. Another tradition that was going to hell once Maya left.

It didn't take them long to settle down. Ignoring their questions about why she wasn't getting ready for bed with them, Tess put glasses of water and aspirin capsules on both bedside tables, turned on James Blake's second album that they all liked to fall asleep to, and left the house.

She didn't lie to herself about where she was going when she grabbed another Uber. Club Bang-Cock was still crowded when she got back, the lines non-existent since it would close in less than an hour.

Tess approached the hostess station, cautiously smiling at the thick-hipped girl with the lipstick that was still flawless at the end of the night.

"Excuse me," she said. "Can you tell me if Alex is done for the night?"

The girl looked her up and down, a smile of pity on her face. "I'm afraid we don't divulge any information about our servers or dancers." She obviously dismissed Tess as one of the thirsty women whose tame wet dreams featured the boys of the club and who wanted to make those dreams a reality.

In a way, Tess was glad it was hard to get to Elijah, that meant strange women didn't have unrestricted access to him. But she wasn't like them, she just wanted… What exactly? She couldn't exactly tell the hostess that Elijah had been the only one who wanted to see the real her in…forever. That, like her mother had before she died and took the last of Tess's childhood with her, he had looked at her and seen behind the careful mask she had constructed over the last eight years.

Tess shook her head, trying for her her least embarrassed smile. "Never mind. Thanks, though."

The hostess nodded back and went back to the ledger she'd been looking at before Tess walked up. Now what? Since the last thing she wanted to do was go home to her empty studio apartment in Little 5 Points, she fought through the crowd to wander back into the club where a dancer was finishing up his routine onstage to rousing applause of the audience. It wasn't Alex.

But she watched one of the servers disappear into an "employee only" area curtained off from the rest of the club, dipping beyond the curtain as he walked backward, balancing a tray of empty glasses on an upraised hand.

"Excuse me." She interrupted another server before he could disappear past the same privacy curtain. "I'm looking for Elijah…ah Alex. Can you tell me where to find him?"

The man, bulkier than Alex and with a cleft chin, looked her up and down, a lecherous smile firmly in place. "Are you sure I can't interest you in a substitution? Elijah may look like one of us, but he won't give you what you're looking for. But I'll ready and willing, though." His smile widened to show all his teeth.

Behind her, the club noises rose and fell, sounds of laughter, wolf whistles, the MC who spun lively fantasies for the people in the crowd before bringing the dancers on the stage. The dancers themselves, all gorgeous men with strong bodies, compelling faces, and swivel in their hips to start a thousand personal sexual revolutions. This was the background to her want for Elijah. Tess opened her mouth to tell this one "never mind" too.

Another server came from behind the curtain on the other side that must have had a clear "entrance and exit" sign.

"See you all later," he called behind him and brushed past Tess. Then he turned, a frown on his face.

"I thought you left." He'd changed into jeans and a Martin Luther King, Jr. T-shirt. He had a backpack over his shoulder and looked more like a student than a stripper. *Oh my God.* He seemed so young. He smiled then, a private thing meant for Tess alone.

She couldn't help the smile that took over her mouth in return. "I came back."

The server who had propositioned her looked between her and Elijah then shrugged and continued his way past the curtain and into the kitchen. Elijah looked briefly at him then touched Tess's elbow. "We're about to close so there won't be much for you to see here." He transferred his backpack to his other shoulder and touched a hand to the small of Tess's back. "I'll walk you out to your car."

"Okay." What else could she say?

She didn't want to go home. But she didn't quite know what she wanted to do either. He intrigued her in a way that was all escape and fantasy, but she also knew that wasn't the way to look at a life and blood man. His profession wasn't his job, and it sure as hell wasn't his job to provide a fantasy for her.

The noise in the club was too loud for him to say anything to her that she would hear, so Tess only nodded again when Elijah guided her through the crowd and out a side door that took them back out to the alley where they'd talked earlier. Their footsteps tapped quietly in sync, her in her sandals, Elijah in dark Nikes, the night shadowy and intimate around them.

Shit. What was she doing here lusting after a boy that probably didn't even shave yet? But she slipped her eyes over him and her gaze clung to the faint five o' clock shadow, his arms dusted with hair, the thick knob of his Adam's Apple, the width of his shoulders under the T-shirt. Okay. He definitely shaved. And despite what Lisa had said earlier, he had to be at least twenty-one. Other than that, Tess had no idea. She backed around to her original thought.

Jesus, what am I doing here with this boy?

She was so busy contemplating his age that she didn't realize they were almost at the parking lot. The night pressed in on her, hot and sweet. Tessa's skin tingled from where her hand brushed Elijah's as they walked and she tried not to shiver and sigh like a love-struck teenager. But she could no more control her reaction than she could change the composition of the stars.

"So…why did you come back?" he asked as they approached one of the last huddles of cars left in the parking lot.

"I'm not really sure." True, she hadn't been able to forget about his words in the alley, so sure, so mature for a boy who, away from the stage lights, and in simple jeans and a T-shirt, now looked like he should be asking a girl out to senior prom. But her attraction to him was also undeniable. The combination of the strength and beauty of his body, the unexpected wisdom in his eyes, the way he takes to her. And strangely, very strangely the thought that she could allow herself to be weak with him. Plus, she desperately wanted the distraction.

His smile flickered on. "Are you being honest with me?"

"The real question is, am I being honest with myself?" Tess made a derisive sound.

He seemed to take her answer in stride, nodding slowly in time with their footsteps. Near the largest group of cars, he looked around. "Which one is your car?"

Oh, shit. She must have really left all her brain cells back in the club. "None of them. I didn't drive." Tess refused to be embarrassed. She shrugged. "Uber got me here."

"Do you want me to…to drive you home?"

Was that what she'd come all this way for? Another shiver made Tess clench her back teeth and she looked up at him, trying to act like the more responsible one, but the shivery feeling in her stomach wouldn't let her go. To ground herself, she reached for the strap of her purse and realized that she'd grabbed the sides of his T-shirt instead, already committed to a course of action her body knew but her mind was just catching up with, she stretched up, leaned in.

Kissed him.

His mouth was a firm curve under hers. A shocked gasp against the press of her mouth. The shivery feeling in her belly rippled through her body, down to her toes, up to her lips until she sparked with arousal and desire, for him. An impulse. But he wasn't returning the kiss. She drew back.

Elijah's lips had fallen open shock, a parted wet curve, he stared at her with eyes widened to the point of wonder, staring at Tess like he'd never seen her before. Embarrassment flushed her red hot.

Shit. She pulled back and he still didn't say anything, just stared at her with his oasis eyes.

Tess backed away. "I'm sorry." The shivery feeling fled for the hills leaving her cold and awash in humiliation. "That was stupid of me." God, he must think she was some sort of desperate cougar. "Shit!"

He reached out to her but she kept moving back, gripping her purse for real this time and quickly scanning the parking lot to see if anyone saw her shame. Another desperate woman trying to sleep with a stripper before going back to her boring life. Oh God…

"No—It's not that," Elijah said, a hand still held out, fingers opening and closing in the air. He looked confused. Surprised. But the look seemed to be turned inward. I don't—"

But the last thing Tess wanted was for him to feel sorry for her. She was the one who just slobbered all over him like a desperate poodle begging to be loved. "It's okay. I just made a complete fool of myself." Fuck. And earlier she thought the day couldn't get any worse.

Tess pulled herself back together. Smoothing a hand down her blouse over her belly, taking a deep breath, and scrubbing all emotion from her face. She took another step back and was about to turn away when Elijah gripped her elbows and towed her back into the hard warmth of his body.

"Don't do that." He kissed the side of her mouth, a whisper of touch that stole her breath. "Don't keep yourself away from me. You took me by surprise."

Another kiss, still light, still dry, but longer, firmer. His hands skimmed up to her arms, her shoulders. "That's all." His mouth touched hers again, a firmer kiss, a flicker of his tongue along her lower lip.

Desire licked between her thighs and she shivered.

"Tess." Then he was breathing her name against her mouth, and that had been one thing she could never resist, a man calling her name while he tried to make her feel good. She melted under the onslaught of his kisses, sighed when she felt the press of a car door at her back. It was warm from the sunlight of the day. She melted between the hard steel of the car and the muscled plane of Elijah's chest.

"What are you doing?" she asked, her voice sounding drugged even to her own ears.

"Kissing you." He pressed his mouth just beneath her jaw, his breath a furnace at her throat. "I admit I don't have much experience but I was hoping my kiss would be fairly obvious."

"You don't have to…" she tried to find her words but it was harder than it should have been. "…you don't have to do this. I—" The moan she couldn't contain slid past her lips and into the air.

"I want to." Elijah whispered her name again, and the vibration of it settled into Tess's skin.

And she gave up every ounce of her already faint resistance. Sighing, she slid her arms around his neck and leaned into his kisses that were oddly chaste and dirty at the same time, his tongue licking at the seam of her lips, stealing the response from her while his body remained still against hers but practically vibrating with the desire to move.

Tess opened her mouth and licked the sweetness of

his lips, breathed into him and sucked on his tongue. He responded with a deep groan, his tongue sketching desire along the outline of her lips then sliding between to lick and tease, dragging sounds from Tess that she'd never heard before.

He didn't touch her beyond the tight grasp of his hands on her waist but still made her feel like all her brains were leaking from between her legs. It drove Tess mad. She slid her thighs together, her wet panties dragging along her clit. She was ready to give him anything, allow him to yank down her pants, rip her underwear, and plunge into her in front of whoever else cared to look. She was past lust, past coherence, past thought.

Fuck me, she thought frantically. Then realized she said it out loud when he gasped and gripped her harder. His fingers sank into her back, just above the curve of her behind and she curled into him, her body alight with lust and dripping wet. She was past subtlety.

"Do you have a place we can go?" she panted into his mouth, desperate for the completion his kisses promised.

He hesitated. "I…I have a roommate."

The fog of lust lifted for a moment for her to think more coherently. "My place then?" She swallowed and only just stopped herself from grinding into him although the lick of flame in her belly ached to be stoked with more direct contact from his body. Lust carved her wide open and her body clutched at the emptiness, aching to be filled. "It's not far."

She felt his hesitation again, and it wasn't even that he didn't want her, she had the proof of his desire pressed against her belly, thick and tempting, but his muscled arms trembled under the tight clutch of her hands like he was trying to hold himself back.

"Okay." He panted again, pulling away from her. But she followed his mouth for another wet and desperate kiss. She felt the twine of his tongue around hers all the way through her body and between her legs, the slick and agile movement of it, promising all kinds of things that made her sob.

"Okay," she echoed and slipped into the passenger seat of his little Nissan after he opened the door for her, her legs shaky and all her finer thought processes lost to desire.

"Where do you live?" It took Tess a moment to summon enough brain power to remember her Little 5 Points address. "I know where that is," Elijah said. And he sped toward her little apartment like he'd taken her home a thousand times before.

Then they were at her place, fumbling out of the seat belt and across the small paved lot, up the stairs, then her key pushing clumsily into the lock. She dropped the key twice and on the third time, he took it from her.

"Let me." And he slid the key in, a firm thrust and twist of his large hand that shouldn't have been a surprise but it was.

Inside the apartment, she dropped her bag, he dropped the keys and grabbed her by the waist, fingers digging with desperation into her hips. His breath was an excited pant at her ear.

"I can't believe I'm doing this," he groaned into her mouth.

She dragged him by the belt loops past the curtains separating the rest of the little studio from her sleeping area, excitement building inside her with each step. Elijah dropped easily onto the bed when she pushed him, his look wild-eyed and hungry. Tess quickly got rid of her clothes while he tore his off, squirming out of his jeans and shirt on the bed in a way that should have been funny but wasn't. When Elijah was gorgeously naked, his hard and muscled body beautiful by the light streaming in through the window, she practically jumped on him in the bed.

Their flesh slid together and it was electric, a sizzling connection that made Tess gasp in reaction. Elijah's eyes widened and he licked his lips, falling back into the bed with a groan of appreciation, his gaze hungry on Tess' body.

He was a visual feast. Hard everywhere, young and strong, practically hairless but built like an athlete with his wide shoulders, trim waist, and thick thighs that her teeth ached to bite. His dick lay thick and wet-tipped against his belly. A mouthwatering sight. And it was big, bigger than any she'd seen in a long time. Desire dripped from between her legs, insistent and slick. She grabbed his hand and made him feel.

His eyes rolled back in his head, and he made a low and helpless sound that went straight between her legs. Then he looked at her, the gravity and desire equally strong in his gaze. "I haven't done this before," Elijah said, his voice confessional and low in a way that made Tess want to lick him everywhere. "But I'll try to make this good for you, I swear." He petted her wet pussy, a surprisingly fumbling move that still managed to turn Tess on even more. She dropped her own hand low to return the favor. Fuck, he even *felt* big. Silken and hard between her fingers, the leaking slit a pleasure beneath the stroke of her thumb. He whimpered for her, biting his lip when she stroked his dick again.

Tess untangled her thoughts from the addictive sounds he made and the way they made her feel—desperate with lust—to respond to what he'd just said. "I don't usually go home with strangers either." She groaned and touched him again, squeezed him in a gentle fist. "This is a first for me too."

His fingers on her clit between her legs robbed her of the next words. "No. This." He moved his fingers again, a clumsy grope. "Sex." He paused. "With another person."

"What?" Panting, she pulled back, staring hard at his face for some sign he was joking. No way someone this fine was a virgin.

He whined with obvious disappointment when she stopped touching him, his throat moving with a hard swallow. "I—hope…I hope it's not a deal breaker." His hips moved under the startled grip of her hands, a frantic, jerking motion that now made sense if what he said was true. No experienced man would allow himself to seem so eager, so desperate for it, in front of a woman he just met.

But *was* it true? Could a hot man who took his clothes off for hundreds of horny and available women multiple times a week actually be a for-real virgin? The thought was mind-boggling. Impossible.

Then Elijah's dick bobbed in front of her, drooling from its fat and mouthwatering head and blew away every trace of hesitation and disbelief she had. Tess climbed higher up on his body, pressing his dick flat against his stomach with the wet ache of a pussy. The firm heat of him between her lower lips lit a glowing pleasure from her belly up to her hard nipples through to her fingers and toes.

Virgin or not, he felt *fucking* amazing.

"You're much too delicious to give up." Tess rolled her hips again, and his breath audibly stuttered. "But it does change how we'll do things. Only a little, though." And she made sure he was watching as she moved slowly down his body.

Elijah's eyes went wide then he froze against the sheets. "What…what—"

She replied with a stroke of her tongue along the thick vein at the underside of his dick, and his entire body shuddered at the same moment that he grunted like he'd been punched in the stomach. Her thighs shuddered at the sound, her pussy dripping even more. He was so responsive, so open with his reactions to her hands and tongue that it felt like he pushed a slick finger inside her and rubbed her clit at the same time. Tess moaned around his dick, pushed her hips down into the mattress to chase her own pleasure.

The taste of him was almost flavorless. Salt and wet. A silken firmness on her tongue. He'd showered after his night at work and the scent of a generic soap, maybe Ivory or Irish Spring, lingered in the crisp pubic hair and the tender skin under her nose.

With her mouth on him, she was grateful when his hands fisted in the sheets on either side of his hips instead of in her hair. His hands tensed when he sat up to watch her, breath coming quickly past his parted lips, her name punching on each exhale from his mouth.

"I'm gonna—I—I can't—"

Tess stroked his belly, hummed around the thickness of his dick to let him know it was okay. This was what she wanted to happen. Sighing in pleasure, she raked her nails down his chest and across a nipple, her other hand tender on the heavy weight of his balls. He shouted her name as he came, and she pulled off just in time, gripping the twitching length of his dick as he spurted thick and hot over her lips, chin, and throat.

He groaned her name again, his voice rough from shouting. "You're amazing." Reaching down, Elijah wiped her mouth with his thumb. Like a typical man, he cleaned the spunk off his finger with her sheets.

Tess caught his wandering thumb with her teeth. "We're just getting started, baby."

It didn't take long to get him hard again. Slow kisses and rolling in the sheets with him, the wonder in his face as he touched her and learned her body. Tess let him caress her everywhere he wanted, his touches getting more confident, more demanding as the night grew around them.

"Like that?" He breathed the question, his fingers stroking her clit the way she directed, his urgency curtailed since he'd already come.

Tess shivered, his fingers moving over her wet flesh, gushing more wetness from her, her thighs falling wider around his hips as he nuzzled her breasts, fingered her steadily toward an orgasm. She sank her nails into his back and the breath sobbed from her throat.

"Does this mean you need to take the edge off too?" He laughed into her throat.

"As if…uh…you could," Tess challenged although she could barely talk with the familiar pleasure tightening by degrees in her belly.

But she didn't have time to grade him on a curve. After having her mouth on him, nearly an hour of kisses with her pussy getting wetter with each stroke of his fingers and each masculine groan that echoed in the close quarters of her room, her desire had grown to a nearly unbearable level.

"I need you to fuck me," she gasped.

He looked shocked for a moment. Then, "Okay. Okay." He reached for one of the condoms she'd put on the bedside table earlier and pressed it into her hand. "I want you to do it."

Tess tried to ignore the way her hands trembled rolling the condom over him, his dick twitching and thick between her fingers. Elijah's mouth hung open as he watched her, his head tilting up from the bed.

He groaned and thrust up into the loose grasp of her hand. "That feels—that feels good."

Tess climbed on top of him, his hard and lightly furred thighs rasping against her skin, masculine and firm in a way that made her shiver. The way he lay beneath her, eyes glazed with lust, his mouth wet and open as she writhed on top of him, painting his abs with the wetness from between her legs—God!—it was like a drug. He didn't grab her and shove her under him to start pounding into her like most men would have. Instead, he submitted breathlessly to her pleasure, waiting for her take what she wanted.

"Tess—"

His voice choked off when she gripped him. His fingers dug into her thighs, desperation written in the sweat coating his skin, the tight and heaving muscles in his belly.

"Let me..." Tess whispered.

Her thighs burned as she hovered over him, his

hardness at her entrance, then slowly, slowly swallowed him with the wanting slickness of her pussy.

"Jesus…" He arched back in the bed, his eyes tightly closed for a moment before they flew back open like he didn't want to miss a single second of what was happening between them.

He felt so firm, so right inside her.

Elijah's eyes held and met hers, refused to let her go as she started to move on top of him, around him. "I think—" He groaned and bucked his hips, slamming up into her with a motion that made them both gasp. "—I think I might love you."

Tess laughed around her own helpless noise. "It's just…the sex talking." Then she couldn't talk anymore, swept away on the tide of feeling, her breath lost, the pleasure rolling everything else aside.

I might love you too, was her last thought before losing all coherence, her body riding toward pleasure, leaning forward so each thrust stroked her clit and made wet and urgent sounds. Then she was quickening, burning, and spectacularly falling apart.

Through the storm of her own orgasm, she felt him come inside her, his face caught in a look of shock as the room filled with his shouts of pleasure. Tess rode him through the unsteady orgasmic jerks, squeezing him with her internal muscles and prolonging the waves of bliss undulating through her body. When she could eventually move, she climbed off him and dropped back onto the bed.

"God…" Her hand slapped wetly against her sweat-soaked stomach.

"You shouldn't take the lord's name in vain." Elijah only sounded a little like he was joking.

"What are you, a priest?" Tess watched him strip off the condom, resisting the urge to help him with the obviously unfamiliar task. But when he looked around the room for the trash, she took the condom from him, tied it off then dropped it in the small trash can she kept just under the bed.

"Just about," he said, sinking down next to her.

She rolled her head to look at him. "What do you mean?"

The moonlight poured through the window and moved over his face, keeping the hard planes of his chest hidden in almost-shadow, an irresistible temptation for Tess' hands. He pushed into her touch but looked briefly away from her, depriving her of the melting darkness of his eyes. But only for a moment.

"Most of the men in my family are in the church. I was supposed to be a pastor." Despite his confession, he sounded almost…relaxed. His limbs were stretched out toward every corner of her queen-sized bed, but strategically making room for her, and a faint smile shaped his mouth. *First time sex endorphins, maybe.* In the past, Tess had found herself leaking unnecessary confessions a time or two after good sex.

"Is that why you've never…" She gestured mutely to their naked bodies.

"Yeah." He said, then sighed when she soothed him with a long and slow caress down his side and along his hip. His skin was like silk under her fingers. "My parents advised me to do it years ago and, even when I started to want other things, I never found a good enough reason to sleep with anyone."

Tess felt her curiosity reaching out like tendrils

toward him despite the earlier warnings she'd given herself.

"I don't think I've ever met a male virgin over the age of ten before you." She traced the long and uncalloused fingers of his hand, the rhythm of the touches lulling her into an odd combination of relaxation and arousal. His skin was so damn addictive. "And I definitely never met one who was a stripper."

"We don't always get what we expect," he murmured in turn. "I certainly wasn't expecting to end up here tonight." He said it like it was an understatement, his eyes running lazily over her in a way that made her very aware of every place they touched.

Tess breathed into the faint arousal she already felt, allowing it to catch fully alight on the flicker of desire in his eyes. Her nipples tightened. Her hips shifted. Elijah was gorgeous and, before him, it had been a long time since she'd had a man in her bed. But she resisted the flames of renewing desire.

"Why lose your virginity now?" She squirmed and adjusted her body on top of his into a less sexually available position, resting her chin on top of her clasped hands and on his chest. "Why me?"

Yes, he was handsome and in the prime of his youth, but those were reasons for her to want him, not the other way around.

"I don't know," he said far too casually. But the way he said it made her think that he did know. That although he'd just shared his body with her, his thoughts and reasons for ending up in her bed were still his to keep. "Tonight just happened." He tipped his head toward her. "What about you, why did you bring me here?"

Because you're hot. The dismissive comment was within easy reach, but she chose to give him the truth instead. "I couldn't stop thinking about what you said back in the alley. I couldn't stop thinking about you."

Elijah grunted in response, his gaze shifting to look over Tess' shoulder. But she doubted he was seeing into the shadowed corners of her little three room apartment.

"You were on my mind too," he said after a while. "I'm glad you came back to the club."

At the mention of the club, her mind went back to the question that popped up earlier but she'd been too distracted to ask. "Yes, the club where you, the almost-priest, is stripping."

"Pastor not priest." He sighed and shifted against the sheets, looking uncomfortable before his features and his body settled. His lashes fluttering down to fan against his cheeks, the moonlight falling over him and turning him into a Dahomey sculpture. "It seems off, I know. But I made peace with it a long time ago. I don't do anything with the women there. I just dance, serve some drinks and go home alone." He turned to look at her with a shy almost smile. "Until tonight anyway. I need the money, and this pays better than any fast food joint or coffee shop I checked out before. It's my last resort to get where I need to go."

Tess allowed his explanation to just be. It wasn't her place to question him, not when her own reasons for doing things—or *not* doing them—were flimsy at best. "And where do you need to go?" she asked, allowing that least bit of curiosity free rein.

"Away from here."

Tess absorbed that in silence. It seemed that

everyone had a real goal to leave the city, everybody except for her. Something in her face must have given away her unpleasant thoughts because he reached for her, hands sliding down to caress her hip.

"This conversation has outlived its usefulness, don't you think?" He squeezed her butt, an endearing mix of a caress and a grope, her sigh becoming a gasp of arousal when his fingers dipped between her cheeks to the dampness still between her thighs.

Tess tilted her head up to receive his kiss, her legs falling open to welcome the heat flickering stroke of his fingers. "I absolutely agree."

Chapter 2

Tess woke up as sober as when she went to sleep. And just as naked. She shifted in the bed and groaned at the slight soreness between her legs and the unfamiliar brush of a bare body against her own. Sunlight spilled through the windows she kept open, its warmth falling over her bare thighs and hips while the strange man heated the rest of her. Not a strange man.

Elijah.

The night came back to her in quick, pulsing flashes. Her eagerness to have Elijah. The way his uncertain touches and desperate sounds spurred her tenderness, until he took her, a fast learner, heeding her gasped instructions until she was breathless and only moaning her pleasure into the sheets. He was a very good student.

But now he had to leave.

Tess rolled over and slowly pulled away from him, ignoring her own sigh of disappointment. He was sprawled on his belly, the light she loved falling over the hard plane of his back, his ass, and thick thighs. She swallowed hard as her gaze lingered over him, and it was all too easy to remember how all that skin felt under her hands, under her mouth.

This is not the time.

Tess slid out of the bed and picked up his clothes. His jeans with the heavy weight of his keys in them, the T-shirt, his plain white briefs. Her hands flexed in his clothes and she unconsciously brought them to her nose. Clean sweat and a crisp, citrus cologne.

Shit.

There was nothing virginal about him as he lay in her bed, naked with marks from her fingernails carved down his back and across his round ass. The breath left her throat in a hiss as she realized what that really meant. Last night was his *first time.*

With dawning guilt, she remembered her own first morning after. The vulnerability she'd felt after sharing her body for the first time, her discomfort until the boy —her first college boyfriend—had taken her out for breakfast and spent the rest of the day with her, making her feel special. Treasured. The clothes fell from her hands in a tangle at the foot of the bed, Elijah's car keys thudding dimly through the jeans against the hardwood floors.

If her boyfriend had kicked her out after taking her virginity, she'd have felt awful. Like what they shared was meaningless. Tess cursed again. Maybe she should offer Elijah some coffee before he left. Wait… Did she have any coffee? A rustle of the sheets brought her attention back to the bed.

"Hey." Elijah watched her with sleepy eyes, his head cradled on her pillow.

"Hey…" She fought the urge to check the corner of her mouth for drool because…damn.

She saw him look down to the clothes at her feet. "Is this where you throw me out?" Elijah asked.

Yes.

But she shook her head, quickly becoming lost in the crooked smile, the eyes that invited her back to the bed. She was moving back toward him before she gave her body permission to move, ready to climb back into the sheets with him and see if he tasted as delicious as he looked first thing in the morning.

"Do you want some breakf—" She broke off at the sound of her doorbell.

Who the hell?

She looked toward her door the same time Elijah did, a door only separated from where he lay by a few paltry feet and the thin curtain that was her token attempt at keeping the sitting area of her studio separate from where she slept. And apparently fucked strange men she picked up in strip clubs. A quick glance at her phone told her it wasn't even nine yet.

The door bell rang again.

"Tess, we know you're in there. Your car is in the parking lot!" Familiar cascading laughter came from outside her door. Lisa. And maybe even Maya and Tam too.

Shit.

Tess backed away from the bed and grabbed her robe. As she hurriedly belted it, Elijah sat up and she lost precious seconds staring at his hard chest, his abs, the soft but still impressive length of his dick against his thigh.

Oh…

The sound of the key turning in the lock pushed her

away from the bed and had her rushing past the partition.

"I'm coming!" she called out, but it was too late.

She burst through it just as Lisa, along with Maya and Tam tumbled into her apartment, looking very well-rested and cheerful for three women Tess had left in a drunken heap the night before.

"You took too long to—" Lisa stopped and stared.

Tess tightened her robe out of reflex and looked down at herself, seeing no reason for the stunned look on her friends' faces. But they were still staring. She darted a look over her shoulder expecting to see the closed curtain to the sleeping area but instead the curtain had snagged on the arm of the rocking chair giving a clear view of Elijah. Naked.

"What the fuck, Tess?"

Her friends were all getting an eyeful of the man she'd deliriously fucked last night. Quickly, Tess freed the end of the curtain and it dropped back into place, hiding Elijah from sight. But the damage had already been done.

Lisa pointed toward Elijah with a vicious stab of her finger. "You fucked our *stripper*?"

Tess wanted to focus on what her friends were saying but the frantic rustling behind her snagged her attention. In seconds, Elijah burst from behind the curtain, mostly dressed in his jeans, the T-shirt jerking down over his bare stomach, underwear and socks balled up in one hand as he headed for the door where his backpack and shoes lay haphazardly on the floor. He threw Tess a speaking look she couldn't interpret.

"Good morning, ladies."

Tess' friends stared at him with their mouths hanging open. Watched him shove his feet in his tennis shoes, throw his backpack over one shoulder and dash out the door after a quick wave and "talk with you later" at Tess.

Tam was the first one to speak. "Wow, that was unexpected." She looked around the room, briefly met Tess' gaze before making a point of yanking open the windows and letting in the morning breeze. Right. The smell. Tess felt her face grow hot but refused to look away or act embarrassed. She re-tied the fastening to her robe and blew out a breath, heading for the kitchen.

"You guys want some coffee?"

"Yeah, sure." Tam put her bag down on the micro loveseat in what Tess had creatively called the living room, a space with an easy chair and close-up view of the flat screen television mounted on the wall.

"What we want is a damn explanation," Maya said, following her into the large kitchen that was easily half of her studio space. "Did you seriously sleep with our stripper-waiter from last night?"

"I did, Maya. And it's fine." She'd never done anything like this before and Tess could see the shock of it all over her friends' faces. "No big deal."

"Jesus Christ, Tess." Lisa stood in the kitchen with her hands on her designer-clad hips, looking surprised, angry. And jealous. "Is he even legal?"

Even though they none of them said anything about the coffee, Tess set about making enough for four. She put on the coffee pot, pulled out four mugs along with cinnamon, cayenne pepper, and honey. The smell of brewing coffee filled the kitchen.

It seemed easier to address Lisa's comment. That

one rankled the most. "You weren't worried about that when you were planning on sleeping with him yourself."

"Is that what gave you the idea to do it? Did you fuck him and imagine you were me?"

Tess did blush then, but it was a blush of anger, her entire body lighting up with the fiery red of it. "No," she said, her voice sharp as a blade. "Unlike you'd have, I waited until I got him here to jump on his dick."

Maya drew in a shocked breath. "Tess!"

Lisa looked like she wanted to fight, designer clothes and early morning be damned.

As usual, Tam was the first one to recover her equilibrium. "Girls, this is no big deal, like Tess said. We should be glad she found somebody to distract her from all the shit she's got going on."

On cue, Tess' phone rang from the cordoned off bedroom, playing her sister's ring tone.

"Fuck," Tess groaned, turning away her friends.

The marble countertop was hard and cold under the grip of her fingers. She wasted half a moment wondering what would've happened if she accepted Elijah's wordless invitation to get back into the bed, ignored her friends and just indulged in the mindless joy of fucking without worrying about the next hour, the next day. But the half a moment quickly passed. "I'm so sick of everything right now."

"Tessie?" She flinched when Maya gently touched her back. "Is everything okay?"

Tess turned around with the smell of coffee filling her nose, the scent of her friends' distinct perfume in her small apartment, one of the last times she would experience the familiar mix of smells. Tears pricked at her eyes and she squeezed them shut.

"No, Maya. Everything is *not* okay." She opened her eyes and allowed the tears to fall. "You're leaving Atlanta, and leaving me, in a few days. My sister is draining everything out of me, including my money. And I can't steal a night away from the bullshit without y'all getting on my ass about it."

The tears were like acid on her cheeks, a sign of the weakness she'd been trying to hide from her friends for weeks. Years.

"Tess…" Maya came toward her with hands held out like she was trying to soothe a wild animal, and Tess tried not to flinch.

"I can't do this anymore," she said. "I just can't."

Chapter 3

Elijah hadn't meant to have sex with Tess. One minute she was another thirsty woman he had to flirt with for tips, and the next she was a person. A beautiful person with soft and damaged insides and an effective mask to cover it all up. If he hadn't seen that mask slip, he wouldn't have thought about her twice. He wouldn't have been left wondering about her after she left the club. He wouldn't have returned the kiss she gave him.

From that one kiss, the lust that barreled through his system and settled like a heavy hand around his dick, impossible to ignore. Over the years, he'd felt dim versions of that lust. For girls at church camp. Women his mother invited over for dinner. Strangers in the street that had him rushing home in shame to milk himself in the shower until his knees ran weak.

What he felt for Tess in the few hours he'd known her was like a sledgehammer to the gut. Vicious and hard. Not that anyone had ever hit him in the belly with something that big, but he could imagine.

With her still heavy on his mind, he turned the key to unlock the front door of his off-campus apartment. His roommate, Delacourt Hamby III aka Trey, looked up from his sprawl on their shared couch, impossibly studying from the heavy physics book on his lap while simultaneously trying to melt into said piece of furniture. He tapped a blue highlighter against the pages of the massive book and looked Elijah up and down, obviously noticing he had on the clothes he'd worn the day before.

"You getting ready to shock me again, Preacher Boy?"

"Not unless you're the delicate and easily shockable type." Elijah walked past Trey and headed to his own room, very aware that he smelled like sex and his clothes were wrinkled from the night spent crumpled on Tess' floor.

Trey laughed and flicked a pencil at Elijah. "Congrats on popping that cherry, Preacher Boy!"

For the millionth time, Elijah regretted spilling his drunken secrets to Trey during his one moment of weakness with alcohol almost six months ago. It was also coincidentally the same night his parents told him they wouldn't pay for his college education anymore. Sometimes Elijah wished he swore.

In his room, he stripped then, hoping stupidly that Tess would call him even though she didn't have his number, he checked his phone.

Of course, she hadn't called. But a familiar number showed up in red as unanswered.

They probably called while I was at work.

It was his fourth missed call from them in less than

two days. Elijah threw his phone on the bed and went to take a shower.

Under the steaming water, Elijah thought of how he ended up in this place. Through his carelessness. With only one more semester left to take his crazy double-major course load, he'd gotten sloppy about trying to hide it. Although strictly speaking, it wasn't his fault his theology professor (and incidental friend of the family) had talked to his father about Elijah's work in the computer science department distracting from his "more important" classes. The distraction had earned him a B+ in Professor Bailey's class instead of the usual across the board A+.

The discovery of his double major—instead of the single Theology degree his parents insisted they pay for —had sent them over the edge. They saw his rebellion as a slippery slope. Once Elijah defied them about his major and getting into the seminary, it was only a short ride to atheism, bisexuality, and getting arrested at Black Lives Matter rallies. Just like the path his brother had taken.

Screw them, he thought with an uncharacteristic flash of anger and bitterness that left him nauseated at himself. But the bitterness was becoming more common as each week passed that he had to take off his clothes for tuition money. Before leaving for college, he'd gotten a job to help pay for school but his parents argued him into quitting, saying he needed to focus on college full time, get his theology degree, and take the collar like so many of the men and women in his family had done.

But that plan was finished now.

Elijah climbed out of the shower, vigorously toweling

his hair dry, his chest, thighs, and back. He flinched when the towel scraped over his back, a raw row of scratches Tess had dug into him the night before. His dick stirred when he turned to look at the scratches in the mirror, memory flashing vivid and hot of how she'd clung to him while he moved between her legs, the hot clasp of her around him as she guided him to his second orgasm of the night, unable to believe the miracle of heat and wet of her, the noises she made and the certainty of her pleasure, feeling her come apart around his dick then his fingers and tongue the same way she had effortless done to him.

Unable to resist, he gripped himself, a firm stroke, and hissed at the bright bolt of pleasure that shot through him. Faint though, compared to what he'd shared with Tess. To what he planned to share with her again. If her friends hadn't come when they had, he was sure they'd still be in the bed now, lust and delectation rolling continuously between them, electric and unstoppable. His eyes fluttered shut.

A chirp from his phone yanked his hand off his dick. What if it was her?

No. Not possible, remember?

Elijah fastened the towel around his waist and picked up the phone. It was his mentor from the computer science department.

"Hello?"

"I'm glad I caught you, Elijah. I have some excellent news." It must have been for Professor Mattson to reach out to him on a Sunday morning.

"Lay it on me, professor."

"The colleague I told you was impressed with the app you designed last semester. He's offering you the job we talked about."

As the words registered, Elijah had to sit down hard on the edge of his bed. The thing he'd worked so hard for was finally coming his way.

"For real?"

"Yes. Contingent upon you graduating, of course."

Elijah released a shaky laugh. "Of course."

"Congratulations, my boy. Once I found out the news, I had to tell you right away. It should make the rest of your time here bearable, knowing that you have a destination and some financial security."

In a fit of self-pity a few months back, Elijah had revealed his parents' sudden withdrawal of financial support to Professor Mattson. His mentor, long impressed that Elijah was tackling simultaneous undergrad and graduate degrees, helped him get a partial scholarship he hadn't even known he was eligible for.

"Thank you, professor. You have no idea. Just… thank you." But those words couldn't convey the slightest bit of what he was feeling. After being abandoned by his parents, he'd felt adrift, his future uncertain. He even thought he'd end up working at the strip club well after school. But now… He drew in a breath that shuddered his entire body. He was so grateful.

"You did all the had work, Elijah. Harder than any student I've had in a long time. I'm happy you're finally reaping the rewards."

Once he hung up, Elijah could only stare at the phone in amazement. *Damn.*

As much as he prayed these days, this job was the answer to his prayers. He needed the distance from his parents and from the hurt he felt at their abandonment. Knowing they pushed him away to not deal with the same emotional turmoil their brother's life choices put them through didn't make him feel any less angry. Or betrayed.

At the thought of his older brother, Elijah reached for the phone again. But he wasn't ready to talk to Caleb yet. Not when the blame against his brother for what his parents had done sat so heavily on him. Instead, he finished getting dressed, intending to share the good news with Trey. Relentless teasing aside, Trey was a good friend. He was the one who'd hooked Elijah up with the gig at Club Bang-Cock. If it wasn't for him, Elijah would probably be looking forward to sleeping in a cardboard box next semester.

He pushed open his bedroom door, a grin on his face and relief bubbling up in his chest. "Guess which preacher boy got a job after graduation?"

Chapter 4

After his classes the next day, Elijah went to find Tess. With his heart drumming in his chest, he lurked in her apartment parking lot, sipping from a Styrofoam container of gas station coffee and hoping she showed up before someone called the cops on him. He felt conspicuous and desperate.

The coffee wasn't bad and the day was nice enough, but that didn't stop his sigh of relief when her little gray Honda pulled into the parking lot. Even through the windshield of the car, he saw the widening of her eyes, the caution as she brought the car to a stop and got out. She looked tired.

He held up his hands before she could say anything. "I'm not stalking you, I promise."

She looked incredible in her work clothes, her lush figure on display in the gray blouse and black skirt, an ID badge hanging conspicuously from her waist. Despite her tiredness, she looked ready to murder him with her fierce gaze and his belly clenched tight, the sudden memory of her, hot and wet around his throbbing dick, nearly making him embarrass himself.

Elijah cleared his throat and shoved his hands in his pocket, never happier that his briefs were tight and his pants loose.

"If you're not stalking me then what are you doing here?" Tess shouldered her practical gray purse and firmly closed her car door.

"Coffee?"

She tilted her head toward his bright red coffee cup. "I think you've already got that covered."

He tossed the cooling brew behind him in the dirt. "I'm empty now."

Her eyebrow rose and a faint smile curved the corners of her mouth. "Were you this ridiculous the other night?"

"You don't remember?" He challenged her with a look and a smile of his own.

"I remember *everything*."

Elijah's entire body flushed hot and he swallowed the thick rise of lust as she watched him with all the knowledge of what they'd done together on her face.

"And you want to…have coffee?" More teasing in her voice, a higher tick of her eyebrow.

"Yes." At the very least. He was a confused ball of feeling, mostly lust and fascination. The night before, he'd given up on his self-imposed moratorium on masturbation and indulged in thoughts of her, of them, until he spilled himself to gasping, and then into sleep.

"Okay," Tess said hoisting her bag higher on her shoulder. "Let's go get that coffee then."

He fell into step beside her, hands still in his pockets and held his tongue while they crossed the parking lot and ended up on the small side street. She was so small. Somehow he'd forgotten that. In his memory of that night, she'd been powerful. A strong and sensual creature who'd effortlessly brought him to his knees and to pleasure again and again. But she was no taller than five and a half feet, the top of her head coming only to his chin.

She took him to a small coffee shop nearby. When they walked in, the woman behind the counter greeted her by name and immediately started to make a drink without asking what she wanted.

Elijah looked at the menu, not sure if he was up to drinking any more caffeine that day. What had he been thinking, getting coffee at the damn gas station? Before getting to Tess' place, he'd been exhausted from long hours in the library then in the lab. Even with the coffee he'd had earlier that morning, the weariness dragged at his shoulders and made him want to fall into bed with computer codes scrolling behind his drooping eyelids. But thoughts of Tess wouldn't let his mind to rest. And so, he'd come to her. Already drinking his second massive cup of coffee for the day.

"I'll have what's having," he finally said to the woman behind the counter. He didn't want to waste precious time examining the chalkboard menu for a drink he didn't care about.

Elijah pulled out a twenty and paid for their drinks without giving Tess the satisfaction of denying him that small thing. They took a table by the window.

"That's a hot chai, by the way," she said as they sat down.

Elijah sipped. "It's not bad."

"It's damn delicious," she said with a flashing smile

at the woman behind the counter who chuckled before sinking back down on her stool behind the counter and the book she was reading. To Elijah, Tess gave a less brilliant smile, but the tiredness behind it was obvious. "Why are we here?" she asked.

He bought himself some time by taking another sip of the drink. It was rich and creamy and hot, familiar spices sliding over his tongue, filling his mouth with heat before it slid easily down his throat.

"I want to see you again," he finally said.

She flicked him a cynical look. Something of the mask she'd worn in the alley the night they'd met. "Really? Or do you want to fuck?"

The unexpected vulgarity sparked a flicker of something down Elijah's spine. Usually, something like that turned him off. Instead, he was steadily hardening in his jeans. Under the table, he spread his legs wider to give himself some room.

The bell above the door jangled when someone else walked into the otherwise empty coffee shop, but he didn't pay it much attention. Tess smirked across the table at him while the heat climbed in his face and pooled in his lap.

"That's what you want isn't it?" she pressed. "to take me back to my apartment and…get me into bed." The word "fuck" was heavily implied despite her euphemism.

He didn't bother denying it. "Would that be so wrong?"

"This can't—"

"Elijah Farris?" An incredulous laugh jerked Elijah from the magnetic beauty of Tess' eyes. "I didn't think you left the lab much less campus. What are you doing in a den of iniquity like Little 5?"

Caleb Stewart, his sometimes lab partner and prime asshole, sauntered over to their table, leaving behind the girl he'd walked into the coffee shop with. The girl glanced over at them but turned back to the chalkboard menu without a second look.

"I'm minding my own business." As always, Caleb thought he was joking when he was being rude.

He laughed and dropped a heavy hand on Elijah's shoulder. "Looks like some hot business, too."

Caleb turned a sly grin to Tess who gave him a look that would freeze fire. Caleb took a stumbling step back. "I'll uh…leave you to it."

After he walked away, Tess turned the same look on Elijah. She grabbed her coffee the same moment that she stood. Her chair scraped harshly across the floor, yanking Caleb's gaze and that of the woman behind the counter, toward them. "You're seriously a student? Not even a college graduate?"

But she didn't wait for him to answer. After managing an abbreviated wave at the woman behind the counter, Tess shoved out the door, her hot chai firmly clutched in her hand, her back an unyielding line.

In the chaos of the late evening always present in Little 5, she walked quickly away from him and down the sidewalk, miraculously not spilling a drop of her drink. He winced when his own chai sloshed over and burned his hand despite its tightly closed plastic cover. He tossed it in a nearby trash can and ran to catch up with Tess.

He grabbed her hand, gripped harder when she spun to face him. "What are you afraid of?" he asked.

She tried to shake him off. "Nothing! You're a child."

"I'm a man, not a boy."

"Just because you can fuck on the first try doesn't make you a man."

A woman walking past jerked her head to look at them and nearly stumbled on the sidewalk.

Elijah clenched his jaw. "I was a man before that, and that's the reason you fucked me in the first place." The harsh curse word scraped hard and unfamiliar across his tongue but he refused to regret it. Anger and frustration swept away any urge to be careful with his words.

But instead of making Tess pay attention to him, it brought a flash of anger over her features, real and explosive. But she didn't shout at him. Instead, she threw away her chai too and stalked back toward her apartment in an angry click of heels.

This time he didn't chase her. "When are you going to stop running away from life?" he shouted after her instead.

Tess stopped as if she'd run into a brick wall. People walked all around them, some curious eyes rustling at their edges to find out what was going on but it all made Elijah feel like they were nothing more than an improv show. But he wasn't acting. He was done with that, done with performing for other people while he buried his real emotions behind a mask of acceptance.

"Women are a distraction from the life we planned for you." *All right.*

"Study for the seminary." Sure.

"We won't pay for your college anymore." But... *Okay.*

"That's not fair," Tess said long moments later.

"Do you think it's fair for you to walk away from me, force me to give up on the one real thing I've found in my whole life?"

Tess released her breath in a slow hiss. "But I'm a coward, remember? Isn't that what you just said to me?"

Where did that come from? Elijah frowned at the pain revealing itself in her face. "That's what you think about yourself, that's not what I said and you know it."

Tess looked around her, at the trash can where she'd just thrown her drink, regret wrinkling her nose and baring her teeth. "Fuck." She looked anywhere but at him, then released another sigh, a decision apparently made.

"I'm heading home to make dinner. Do you want to come up?"

She didn't have to ask him twice. Elijah tried to play it cool when he accepted her invitation but his heart was sprinting in his chest, beating fast enough to fly out of his body and race them back to the apartment.

Her apartment was both everything and nothing like he remembered. The night they slept together, everything had been overwhelmed with the look and scent of desire. He couldn't separate the sight of her open front door from the way she'd felt pressed against it. Couldn't parse the faint traces of incense from the drugging scent between her legs. The interior, small enough to easily have been the size of his childhood bedroom, also rang in memory with the sounds of her dizzying moans, the frantic slide of her hand down his pants to cup his aching dick and free it to the warm air. He licked his lips and swallowed.

Tonight, it was just an apartment though. Elijah closed the door behind them, his heart still beating madly in his chest while she walked ahead of him to put away her bag on an antique looking coat rack that held at least a dozen other leather and cloth handbags. Her shoes rapped against the floor as she kicked them off, then picked them up to take them through a door he assumed led to a closet and the bathroom.

"Would you like a drink?" Her voice came muffled from behind the door.

"Yeah, but don't put yourself out. I'm not really a drinker."

"Not even water?" She emerged from the closet in a loose, silken dress that flattered her curvy body even more than her office clothes had. Or it maybe she just looked good in anything she put on. Her hair was still caught in the thick braided crown on top of her head.

Tess brushed past him, the cloth licking briefly at his legs, and headed to the kitchen. Like a thrall, he followed.

"Water sounds good," he said. Although to be honest he would have gladly drunk up whatever she put in front of him.

Her kitchen was surprisingly spacious, fitted with stainless steel appliances, and was wide and airy with the open window letting in the breeze from the approaching evening. Tess poured a can of sparkling water for him then began pulling vegetables from the crisper.

"So, young *man*." She emphasized the second word. "You wanted to talk, so talk."

He shook his head, not about to play that game. "Not like this."

Her mouth twisted into something resembling a smile. "Okay then." She ran a wicked looking knife under the tap and washed a colorful collection of vegetables—carrots, yellow peppers, broccoli—and began to chop them.

"Let's tackle the elephant in the room," she said, not looking at him. "How old are you?"

Of course, she'd go for that one. "Nearly twenty-two." He tried not to make it sound like a confession. "I have one more semester left in school," he said quickly.

"That's a relief. At least you're not a teenager." With the knife paused in the air, she swept her gaze down his body, then shook her head again, most likely chiding herself for falling into bed with someone who just reached the legal drinking age.

"Does this body look like a teenager's to you?" He gestured to himself, knowing she was already paying attention, had already noticed the long swallow she'd taken after looking at him, really looking at him, that first time. Elijah stood with his legs braced wide, hands in the pockets of his jeans to fame the thickness of his dick. He'd done it enough times on stage for it to feel like second nature here in her kitchen. But unlike on stage when he'd done it as a tease, here it was a promise.

Tess pressed her plump lips together. "Lots of genetically modified shit out there masquerading as more than what they are."

He really couldn't help himself. "This is a hundred percent beef. All natural. No hormones, no additives." Well, maybe a few rampant hormones.

She rolled her eyes and went back to chopping the vegetables. Without her asking, Elijah grabbed the things she could need. The wok hanging from the low ceiling next to other pots, soy sauce, salt, and pepper. Udon noodles and coconut milk. It wasn't long before dinner was finished and they were sitting at her small table by the window, their knees brushing and steaming plates of vegetable stir-fry between their elbows.

"You never answered my question from earlier," he said after taking a bite. The flavors of the vegetables along with the coconut milk and noodles was delicious enough to spurt a flash of saliva in his mouth. He couldn't remember the last time he had a home cooked meal. He could fend for himself but rice and black beans didn't compare to the restaurant quality meal Tess whipped up in only a few minutes.

"Would it stop you if I said I didn't want to talk about it?" He liked that she didn't pretend she had no idea what he was talking about.

He shook his head, mouth already open around his fork for another big bite of what she'd made. Tess chewed her own forkful, her other hand resting on the edge of her plate, idly rubbing the corner of the white ceramic.

"I'm not running from anything. I'm just a little… stressed right now." She raised an eyebrow in his direction. "You know, adult things."

Elijah didn't fall for the bait. "The person you were talking to in the alley the other night?"

Her eyes flashed up at him, surprise clear in them. "Yes." She took another slow bite, but Elijah was patient. She seemed to want to talk, or at least wouldn't try to gut him if he asked probing questions. He'd already had his dick inside her, privacy between them at this point was moot. But maybe not everyone thought of sex as intimacy. He'd only done it once after all.

If reluctance had a face, it was hers. "My sister," she said after a silence long enough for him to finish over half his food. "She keeps messing up and I keep bailing her out. I'm trying to break the habit."

Elijah took one final bite of his stir fry before leaning back in his chair. He'd expected her issue to be something…bigger. Something that had to do with a mature man she wanted to be the father of her children or something. But a sister she felt she had to take care of was almost worse. Worse to let go of, or at least in theory. "That's really cool of you to do that. Some people find it real easy to stop caring and cut off every kind of support at the drop of a hat, or at least the second someone doesn't do what they expect."

"Trouble with your parents?" Her tone wasn't sardonic for once.

"At my age, what other kind of trouble is there? Isn't what you want to say?"

She put down her fork. "I wouldn't say that to you. Family is hard, and trouble with them is sometimes the worst kind." On the table, her fist clenched and unclenched. "Most days, I imagine I would have a different kind of life if it wasn't for the responsibility I feel for my sister."

He winced. "That doesn't sound like the kind of support you should be giving. There has to be a balance between being there for the people you love and living the kind of life you want."

"If there is, I haven't found it yet." She nibbled on a piece of broccoli, her gaze far away.

"Maybe you should talk to your sister, find a happy medium for both of you." He shrugged. "Living your life for someone else will only end in resentment and regret."

"It's not as easy as you make it sound," she said.

"Nothing ever is."

Tess shrugged.

And that seemed to be the end of her talking. With her plate only a quarter empty, she stood up from the table. Elijah watched as she grabbed glass containers from the cupboards and began putting the food away, the rest on her plate and the food in the pots. He was about to stand up when she came back to the table, put a hand on his shoulder.

"Don't rush. Relax. I just can't sit and talk about this anymore."

"We don't have to talk about your sister," he said. "There are much better ways to spend the next few hours."

She made a good try at a smile. "Oh, yeah? Like what?"

Elijah grinned and slowly stood up. When she backed away, her eyes widening with interest, he only walked around her with his empty plate and glass in hand. Her quick intake of breath was sensual music to his ears, but he didn't press his small advantage. Hiding his smile, he began to help put the rest of the food away. He'd wanted a second helping of the stir fry, but he wanted to get her into bed more. *If* that was even on the table.

"I'll help with the dishes," he said once all the food was in the fridge and all that was left in the sink was the wok, a pair of cooking spoons, and their dirty dishes and cups.

He washed and she dried. They moved together well in the kitchen, a natural dance he'd his parents do, moving around each other as though knew where each other were but still wanted to touch. As conservative as

Milton and Janine Farris were, they'd never been shy about showing their tenderness for each other. Elijah dragged his mind from the minefield of his memories with a wince.

"What kind of life would you have if you didn't take care of your sister?" he asked, his own pain unconsciously making him reach out toward hers.

She shrugged, accepting the wet plate he handed her.

"There's no point in having those fantasies," she said, drying the plate with a towel. "It just makes real life harder to live."

Elijah couldn't help but laugh. "Says no teenaged boy ever."

"But I thought you weren't a teenager," she said. The plate clinked against the metal dish rack as she put it away.

He barely stopped himself from rolling his eyes. She was making all this unnecessarily complicated. "Everyone has fantasies," he said. "Sometimes it gives us something to aspire to. Sometimes it just gives us something to help cope with an unpleasant reality." He glanced back at her, eying the easy fit of the dress over her sensuously curved body, its drape over her bra-less breasts. "Sometimes it's just fun."

He gave her the pair of forks and he deliberately slid his fingers between hers in the exchange, the wet friction tightening his belly. She tried to hide a smile from him and was almost successful. Elijah drained the sink, cleaned up the spilled water around its edges, and dried his hands. When he turned, she still had the forks in her hands, staring off into space, her lower lip caught between her teeth in an uncharacteristically vulnerable expression.

"Let me help you with those."

He clasped her hands between his and she refocused her eyes with a shudder he felt in the delicate weight of her fingers.

She pulled away with a downward flutter of her lashes. "I can handle a few forks," she said dropping the aforementioned utensils in the dish rack. They clinked softly together.

"Can you?" He waggled his eyebrows and she gave a soft huff of laughter.

"Real mature," she said.

"I said I'm a man," he murmured, crowding her against the counter. "Not that I'm a mature one."

She laughed again, a soft sound that drew him even closer. "That's not a plus, by the way." Her plump mouth was still slightly glistening from their dinner, a shimmer of plum dark lips that made him want to bite and lick at them until she opened up and moaned for him. Arousal pooled in his belly, and lower.

"You make my head spin." He leaned into her, breath huffing past his own parted lips but she turned away from him at the last moment and his mouth brushed her jaw instead.

"I didn't invite you here to fuck me," she said.

There was enough breathlessness in her voice to make him bold. "Why not? Were you trying to save my virtue?"

"We both know it's far too late for that." The words hitched in her throat, breaking her words in half. They were so close, he could feel the thudding beat of heart.

Elijah stroked the line of her throat, the frantic beat

of her pulse. He kissed her there and she shivered into him. Through her dress and his clothes, her body called to him, begging him to revisit the hours they'd spent together a few days before. But he didn't want it to be like it was before. Her teaching him. His clumsy explorations that accidentally stumbled upon her pleasure.

A natural scholar, he'd hit YouTube in the week since that first night. He knew a woman grew wet when she wanted sex, readying herself for the press of his dick or fingers. He grasped Tess' hips, caressed her through the thin cloth. He felt the line of her underwear beneath his palms, the heat of her skin. With a groan, he fisted the cloth and dragged it up.

"What are you doing?" She breathed the question against his throat.

"Giving up the rest of my virtue."

He dropped to his knees and yanked up her dress the rest of the way.

"You don't—" His mouth on her sucked away the rest of what she was going to say.

Groaning, he settled more comfortably on his knees to eat his dessert.

———

Elijah woke up hungry. Sleep gradually slipped away from him and he licked his lips as his entire body woke up, his thighs flexing, hips moving against the sheets, the light touch of the breeze on his dick. He was already hard and leaking. Tess, warm and pliant next to him, moved as he moved, moaned and tilted her head away in sleep when he tried to kiss her.

Right. Morning breath.

During the night though, they'd shared far more intimate things than morning breath. In the wake of sex that left them both exhausted and half the bed soaking wet, Tess talked again about her sister. About the difficulties they had, the things she wanted, the things she didn't want. All of her fears. And Elijah shared with her in turn, revealing his parents' abandonment, the job offer that would take him out of Atlanta, the brother he loved.

He and Tess had broken each other open and, for a few precious and unexpected hours, fit their wounded selves together to create something he'd never experienced before. Something soul-shaking. The entire time they talked, he'd stopped himself from declaring foolish things.

I want you in my life.

You smell like my future.

Leave Atlanta with me.

To stop himself from saying any of these things, Elijah kissed her again.

"You're entirely too awake right now," she groaned into the pillow.

He felt the vibration of her words under his palms as he moved them up her ribs. Her breasts were plump and soft, nipples already hard. She groaned again but for a different reason this time.

"Good morning." He licked the dip between her collar bones.

"I have to go to work," Tess murmured. But her hands were already moving over his back, her nails sinking deliciously into the shifting muscles in a way that made his dick even harder.

"I have to go to class," he said around her nipple.

She shivered against him, her thighs falling open to allow his hand between. The humid thatch of her welcomed the questing length of his fingers.

She was so wet. He groaned long and deep when her wetness sucked him in.

"I'm a good student," he said into her throat, smiling when he felt her stiffen, but only a little. "I've been studying."

Elijah pulled his fingers from the damp heat of her, slid his thumb over the firm flesh.

Clitoris. He remembered from the video he'd watched. He stroked her in the rhythm the video recommended, pushed his hips into the sheets to the same rhythm, groaned when she gasped and opened her thighs wider for him. "I can't miss the opportunity to become better at everything I do."

Her thighs were slick with her lust and he swiped at the dampness with two fingers, then slowly slid them inside her. She bucked against him with a gasp. He kept his thumb on her clitoris, his two fingers curving up and seeking.

"Elijah!"

Right there. He smiled with satisfaction when she jolted under him like she'd been shot with electricity. "Will you let me be a good student for you, Tess?"

"Fuck…" She gripped the back of his head, her neck arching back in the sheets, her hips thrusting in frantic motions into his fingers. She was *shaking.* "Oh my God…" She was falling apart.

His dick was hard enough to drive nails and he wanted desperately to be inside her and satisfy the lust simmering at the base of his spine, an urgent and hot impulse. But he didn't want to stop what he was doing to get a condom, and he didn't want to do something either of them would regret later.

"I want to be inside you so bad." He sucked her nipple into his mouth, one after the other.

Her wetness slicked his fingers even more. Her moans rose higher in the room. "Then do it… Fuck me!" She gasped and twisted under him. Already she glistened with sweat, her hips twisting against the sheets, her nipples wet from his mouth. Her woman's flesh sucked greedily at his fingers.

Jesus…

Her pleas made Elijah wish desperately he was a different person. Wish he would just reach down and slot his dick into her and give them both what they so desperately craved. But he was only himself, so he slid down her body, mouthing at her warm skin, the heaving line of her stomach while moving his fingers inside her, the wetness of her coating his fingers like a miracle, like the best thing he'd ever touched, like the life he'd so desperately wanted for himself so long ago but that was now out of reach. She gasped his name.

She was so succulent, and he was desperately hungry for her.

"Tess…" He latched his mouth to her clitoris, licked it luxuriously, sucked and hummed his pleasure into her skin. He fucked her harder with his fingers. Tess clawed his shoulders and widened her thighs against the sheets.

Oh, Christ. The heat in his belly intensified, and he moved desperately against the mattress, his dick tangled in the sheets and thick enough to burst.

"How…how are you so good at this alrea—oh God!" Her words stuttered off in a wailing cry when his fingers found that spot inside her again.

"You make me want to be good." He lifted his head to groan the words into her furred flesh as his hips desperately moved and dick leaked, fucking into the sheets and chasing friction.

He was driving himself insane, but damn it was so good to touch her. His fingers felt inextricably linked to his dick, to the things he was doing to her, the wetness of her around his fingers, her clitoris in his mouth, the dripping and wet noises of him fucking his fingers into her, all feeding the lust rising in him.

Tess's body clenched tight around his fingers the same moment she cried out, her wet flesh moving in undulating waves against his hand. And that was the very thing that brought him over, the thought of pleasing her so very well. Everything inside him froze. Then exploded in shuddering bursts. His hips jerking beyond his control against the sheets. But he didn't stop moving his fingers, didn't stop feeding her pleasure when he knew she could keep doing this, exploding again and again as long he kept touching her.

"So good…" She groaned and moved under him, the damp flesh of her thigh hot against his arm. "But —" she gasped. "I have to go to work. As much as I'd… love to stay in this bed with you all day…I…have to got to work."

Elijah sucked her clitoris into his mouth again, moved up to lick a nipple, kiss her shoulders. "Call in sick," he murmured into her throat. But he knew he had to go too. If he was going to graduate on time and keep the job he'd been provisionally awarded, he needed to keep going to class, especially his early morning lab.

He gazed down at her while she slowly rode his thigh, painting him with the slick evidence of her pleasure. Her lashes fluttered against her damp cheeks and she was smiling.

Damn. He could look at her forever.

"Okay." Elijah kissed the corners of her mouth and dropped briefly down to lick the sticky cleft between her thighs. "Can I see you tonight?"

"Maybe." He didn't imagine the frown that flickered across her face, worry briefly replacing the passion in those wine dark eyes of hers. She slid from under him and escaped to stand by the bed, showing him the bare curves of her body, all the places he'd touched and licked and bitten. "I'm seeing Maya after work. Wedding stuff."

Tess grabbed her robe from the chair next to the bed and hid her body from him, pushing past the curtain around the bed to go to the bathroom.

Their morning play time was over.

Elijah stared up at the ceiling and listened to the sound of the toilet flushing, then the shower turning on, the rattle of shower curtain pulling open then closed.

Should I stay?

Their first time together, the unexpected appearance of her friends had pushed their morning in a certain direction. But now... He wasn't sure what to do. Then his phone chimed. His alarm letting him know it was time to get up and get ready for class.

Okay.

Making a sound of disgust at the drying mess on his belly and the hairs around his softened dick, he shoved on his underwear and jeans. He doubted she was open to sharing her shower. That would just make them both late.

He quickly got dressed and made sure he had his

keys and wallet. After a moment's hesitation, he poked his head into the bathroom, blinking through the steam to see the outline of Tess' body through the glass shower door.

"I'm heading out." He shouted above the sound of the water.

"Okay," she called back after a moment's pause.

"I left my number on the bed, you know, in case you want to hang out later or something."

"Okay." This time he heard a smile in her voice.

"Okay." Elijah grinned. "Talk to you later."

They didn't end up getting together but Elijah's phone lit up with a text just as he was falling asleep that night.

I *talked with my sister. See you later this week.*

Chapter 5

E lijah was obsessed. How else to explain why he couldn't get Tess out of his mind? And it wasn't just the incredible sex. It was also the way she discarded her masks just for him, a slow unveiling that made him want to promise her everything. And it was her unquestionable strength, the way she still surrendered to him when they were in bed.

Okay, maybe it was a little bit about the sex.

He crossed the street away from the school of theology, hitching his backpack over his shoulder and already thinking about what to say to Tess the next time they met up. He wanted to suggest something normal like a date, maybe dinner and a movie (and, of course, sex). But would she think that was too sophomoric?

"Elijah."

He jerked out of his reverie when he heard a familiar voice call his name. Eyes narrowed, he swept his gaze across the sunlit campus, the magnolia trees, the tall parking deck, the narrow street leading out to the main avenue in front of the school. Then he saw them. His parents.

Shock stopped him where he stood. Elijah's legs wouldn't carry him any further, especially when he realized they were between him and the lot where he'd left his car. But he'd never been a coward. He stiffened his spine and forced his feet forward.

His parents stood together, his mother in a floral dress and heels, a hat shading her sepia face from the sun. His father in gray slacks and a polo shirt, dress shoes. They waited with a determined gravity for him to approach.

"I didn't expect you," he said when he was close enough.

"We've been calling." His mother offered that as the only explanation for her and her husband showing up on Elijah's college campus as if they hadn't basically told him to go screw himself a few months before.

"I know." Elijah pulled his shoulders back, trying to stretch out the sudden discomfort between them. "What can I do for you?"

Ever since he was a child, his parents taught him to speak to them and to others seriously and as an adult. That way of communicating often left no way for beating around the bush.

"We're your parents," his father said at the same time that his mother offered her own pseudo-explanation with a benign, "We'd like to take you to lunch."

It was well past lunch time, edging into the dinner hour with four o' clock mere minutes away. But Elijah had been on campus since seven that morning and wanted nothing more than to be in his own apartment and not deal with this crap.

But despite what happened, they still deserved his respect.

"Where would you like to go?" he asked, keeping his voice painfully polite.

He was still having a hard time computing that they were there, on his college campus, wanting to talk with him. The last time he saw them, it had been Thanksgiving.

"We can't support this decision you made," his mother told him when he had a bite of turkey halfway to his mouth. "We won't."

They'd pulled the rug so thoroughly from beneath his feet that he hadn't been able to finish his dinner, hadn't been able to stay in the house. Instead, he found himself back at the apartment he shared with Trey, unsteady and as close to tears as he'd ever been as an adult.

"Let's go to the place you like the all day breakfast," his father suggested in his grave voice that he reserved for death announcements.

The restaurant he mentioned was within walking distance, which was good because Elijah would probably crash his car if he had to drive someplace right now. His knees felt like rubber, and his mind ran in circles trying to figure out what they wanted.

"Okay."

They walked to the restaurant in silence, broken only when the bell above the door jangled as they walked in, his father holding the door open for his wife and then for Elijah. In moments, they were seated with menus and water.

The restaurant was barely half full, mostly with students and a few faculty Elijah recognized. His Ethics professor sat by the window with a cup of tea and her open laptop. But she was staring out the window onto the street.

"So…" He encouraged his parents to talk after the waitress had come with their drinks and taken their food orders. The awkward silences were making his chest hurt. "We're having lunch. What now?"

Milton and Janine Farris both looked uneasy, exchanging a look that made it seem like they were reading each other's minds. Their discomfort was so obvious that Elijah wondered if they would be able to eat the food they ordered. His mother had ordered her favorite shrimp and grits while his father tried the paella. Elijah only stuck to coffee with the excuse that he'd already eaten. He hadn't.

He warmed his cold hands around the steaming hot coffee mug. Under the table, his knee jumped in a nervous tick he was glad they couldn't see.

"We came to see how you were," his father said, preacher's voice low but carrying in the small space.

But that obviously wasn't it. His mother looked at his father after taking a careful and prim sip of her iced tea. Three slices of lemon floated with the ice in her clear glass.

"We heard a rumor," his mother said. "We were concerned about you."

"It's a little late for concern, isn't it?" Elijah said, then snapped his teeth shut.

No. He told himself that if his parents ever visited him, he wouldn't show his anger, he would pretend what they'd done hadn't nearly broken him. But at that moment, with his nervous knee and stomach full of butterflies, he felt very much like a boy, like an abandoned son. He muttered an apology and punished himself with a hasty sip of scalding coffee.

"One of your cousins said they saw you in a house of sin."

Elijah froze. That was the one thing he didn't expect them to say. "What do you mean?"

"Your cousin, Marva. She said you were dancing on stage for money. Naked."

"Not a house of sin then," he said with a mocking twist to his lips. "Only temptation to lechery." But his heart was beating furiously in his chest. When he'd thought of applying for the job at Bang-Cock, he was 98% certain he wouldn't run into anybody who knew him or his parents, despite the fact that the family had been in Atlanta for at least three generations. Now what?

The boy in him wanted to apologize and tell them he'd quit and find another way to make money, but it was the man in him who spoke up.

"I have to pay for school somehow," he said.

Even though she'd brought it up, his mother drew a shocked breath. "Elijah! You have to stop working there immediately. It's wrong," she sputtered.

He carefully put his coffee on the table and sat back.

"There's nothing else I can do to make the money for my tuition, rent, and graduation on such short notice." Saying that it was their fault it had come to this seemed redundant.

"We'll lend you the money." His father finally spoke up again. "You can't be in that place doing...whatever. It's embarrassing."

"More embarrassing than letting your friends know you chose to stop being my parents on a whim?"

"It wasn't a whim!" His mother protested. "You disobeyed us." The ultimate sin in the Farris household.

But before Elijah could respond to her, his father took his turn. "We're still your parents. Your sinful ways don't change that."

"Tell that to Noah," Elijah said. As far as he knew, they hadn't spoken to his brother in months. He and Noah talked on the phone at least once a week but they went out of their way to avoid discussing their parents. Their love lives—or Elijah's lack of one—and the goings on in their respective cities was plenty conversation to keep them laughing on the phone for hours.

Tess floated to the surface of his mind, as she often did in unexpected moments. Her struggles with own her family and how those struggles stopped her from moving forward and moving on. He didn't want that for her, or for himself. And with that, he's had enough.

"Look," he said. "You don't have to worry about anyone else seeing me at the club." His mother smiled at him in relief and his father nodded as if he'd expected nothing less. "I got a job offer and I'm taking it right after graduation." That was only two months away. "It's not in Georgia so you won't have to worry about seeing me at all."

"What?" His mother darted a look at her husband. "This is the first we're hearing about this."

His parents had connections at various schools and churches in the Atlanta area and had always planned for Elijah to be yet another Farris with firm connections in the Atlanta spiritual community. But Elijah hadn't wanted the same thing they did in a long while, and when he was being honest with himself he could almost admit that them dropping him on the edge of financial desperation had been the best thing they could've done.

"You both left me to fend for myself," he said. "That's what I'm doing."

"But it doesn't make sense for you to leave Atlanta," his mother said. "You don't have people anywhere else."

"I don't have people here either," he said, and took a vicious satisfaction in the flinch that crossed her face. But he immediately felt sorry for it.

Under the table, his fist clenched hard on top of his still ticking knee.

"Elijah, we forbid it," his father said, his voice an authoritarian rumble. "You can't leave the city. God knows what will happen to you out there."

His mother drew in an audible breath. "Unless you're not going to be alone." Before she spoke, Elijah knew exactly what she was going to say and he drew himself tight to steel himself against it. "You're running off to California with your brother, aren't you? You're going to join him in his life of sin out there in that city of devils." His mother's voice rose with each word until she was nearly shouting, attracting the notice of everyone in the restaurant. Her husband's hand on hers did nothing to stop her.

"If I chose refuge with my brother after my parents abandon me, there's nothing wrong with that. He's family, no matter what you think and how you act toward him." Elijah sighed. "I'm tired," he said, feeling that exhaustion suddenly down to his bones, the roots of his teeth. "I've had a long day and I have a project to work on tonight." He took a slow sip of his coffee for want of something non-destructive to do with his hands. "Thanks for coming to see me." He stood up, grabbed a five-dollar bill from his wallet and dropped it on the table, ignoring his father's grumbling protests that he would pay for the coffee. "Tell Marva I said hello."

When he turned to go, his father grabbed his arm. "Son."

Elijah stopped and waited for his father to say something else. But when nothing came, he gently shook off the already faltering grip. "I'll see you guys around."

Then he walked out of the restaurant, swallowed hard at the final-sounding jingle of the bell when the door closed behind him. Pulling out his phone, he wondered if Tess would have time to see him tonight. Would she even care that he'd just broken his own heart all over again?

▭

After hanging up with Elijah, Tess slid her phone into her purse and gave her make-up a brief check in the bathroom mirror. She hadn't needed to go to the bathroom but didn't feel comfortable talking with Elijah in front of her friends, or more to the point, in front of *Lisa*.

A few minutes before, he'd called in the middle of a boozy late lunch at their favorite luxury hotel and something inside her had jumped at the sight of his name on her phone's screen. Without a second thought, she accepted the call and stepped away. He wanted to see her and she wanted to see him. With her heart knocking mad and fast in her chest, she'd said yes.

Lisa wasn't going to like it but *fuck* her.

Her friend hadn't loosened up on her criticism of Tess for sleeping with Elijah the night of the bachelorette party. If anything, she'd gotten even more stubborn and more resentful about it. But her resentment didn't stop Tess from wanting Elijah, or from caring about him.

Their sex was better than good. The best she'd had in a long damn time, and since the first night, Tess couldn't stop thinking about him. His inviting smile and youthful enthusiasm. The feel of him inside her. The late night confessions they shared. It seemed impossible that a stripper, would-be priest, and virgin had ended up in her bed. But he had and she didn't want to let him go.

In the mirror, her face shifted, becoming hard and possessive in a way she'd never seen before. Then she sighed and forced her features to relax. Tess traced another coat of gloss over her lips and turned to leave the bathroom.

Then her phone rang.

"Hey." She greeted her sister in a neutral tone and stepped back from the bathroom door to sink into one of the gold couches in the small ante-room.

They hadn't spoken in almost four days. Despite her initial impulse, Tess never gave Tracy the money she asked for. The approaching reality of Maya's wedding, Elijah's presence in Tess' life, and even her own misgivings were making Tess question her choices where Tracy was concerned. The last time they talked, Tess asked her sister what she would do if Tess left Atlanta. Tracy's answer had been a shrug and a casual, "I'd go on with my life."

That response had stunned Tess to the core. The sister she'd placed above most things in her life wouldn't give a damn if she stayed or left.

"What's up, Tracy?" She prompted after her sister's prolonged silence.

A sigh came at her through the phone. "I…I just want to say I'm sorry. About the other day."

This was new. Her sister never apologized for anything. "About what exactly?"

"Making it seem like I didn't know what you were asking." Another sigh came along with the sound of a sliding glass door. Tracy stepping outside. "I know Maya is leaving town finally and you're not going with her. It…I want to let you know it's okay for you to go. Not because I don't care that you're leaving but because… because it's not right for me to tell you to stay."

Tess frowned down on the plush rug under her feet, tracing its familiar pattern with her eyes until it gave way to swirled marble flooring. "What brought this on?"

More silence. "Tam called me."

Fuck. When would her friends learn to stay out of her business?

But Tess was surprised it was Tam who'd talked to her sister and not Maya. Maya was always meddling. Tam left Atlanta years ago to make a whole new life for herself and her daughter in Miami, and she'd never looked back. But she always encouraged Tess to leave, occasionally sending her job openings from all over U.S. along with some little meme or whatever they called it about courage.

She frowned harder at the rug. "What did Tam say?"

"Nothing I didn't know. The point is, I've been selfish. If you left, I'd miss you, Tessie, but that's better than you giving up stuff just because you can't say no to me."

"I…" Tess really didn't know what to say. Tracy

sounded…mature. Not at all like the demanding and bratty sister she'd gotten used to.

"I'll come by this weekend after the wedding," Tracy said. "We can talk more then. Okay?"

"Okay." Tess agreed in a daze. Then she hung up and made her way back to the lavish, European-style dining room where her friends waited.

They sat around the table, drinks near their hands, all talking at once and laughing.

"Oh, good!" Maya said, the corners of her eyes crinkling with happiness. "We were just talking about you and your boy toy."

Tess glanced briefly at Tam as she sat down. Her friend met her eyes with a telling smile. "Don't you guys have anything better to talk about?" Tess muttered. "Like a wedding?"

"No!" They all spoke at the same time, echoing each other although Lisa looked irritated while Tam and Maya were obviously amused.

"This is big," Maya said. "You've always stayed away from the young ones before."

"Rightfully so," Lisa chimed in, cutting her eyes hard at Tess.

"Stop being such a jealous bitch, Lisa." Tam giggled, the mimosas obviously getting to her already. "You know you'd ride that boy all the way to campus and back if he gave you half the chance."

Maya and Tam laughed while Tess frowned at Lisa.

"Why are you giving me such a hard time about this, Lisa?" *Aside from the obvious?* But Tess didn't say that last part. Her friend's jealousy was as plain as the nose on her face, but that was nothing new. Lisa always had to have the best of everything. The sexiest. If she didn't, she made sure everyone knew how unhappy she was with that state of affairs.

"I'm just worried about you, that's all," Lisa said.

But Tess wasn't buying it. Neither was anybody else at the table if their expressions were anything to go by. And Tess wasn't about to let the problem stealth its way through their dinner and weekend. The wedding was coming up and the idea of having Lisa's bullshit hanging over her best friend's special day didn't sit well with her. She had to be honest and invite Lisa to be the same.

"I'm enjoying this thing with him," she said with an unapologetic shrug. "There's nothing wrong with it. He's young, true. But we're both adults." She raised an eyebrow at her friends. "We're both scratching a mutual itch. No big deal."

"But aren't you afraid you'll get caught up more than you mean to?"

"What does that even mean?" Tess frowned at Maya, trying to see the logic of her friend's question. "I've been afraid for so long, of so many things, that this is actually me *not* being afraid for once. And it feels good. I can't keep living in fear forever."

All three pairs of eyes bugged out at her.

Tam was the one who broke the silence. "But you're the strongest person we know."

Tess ignored Lisa's rude snort. "Don't say that when it's obviously not true. Every test of resilience that comes my way, I fail. I can't keep going like this."

"What are you doing then? Fucking this *boy* to prove to yourself that you can be strong?" Lisa denied the sense of that with a shake of her head. "You're just having a mid-life crisis. There's no other explanation for it."

"Shut up, Lisa." Tam rolled her eyes. "She can't have a mid-life crisis at thirty-four."

"Can I have my own life, though, Lisa? Or do I need your permission?"

"Of course you can have your own life, honey." Maya shot each of the other women a narrow-eyed gaze while reaching across the table to squeeze Tess' hand clenched around the stem of her champagne glass. "What's going on, Tess? What are you afraid of?"

But Maya knew. It was in the vulnerable roundness of her eyes, the way her mouth turned down with a hint of the guilt she'd confessed to Tess only a few weeks before.

I feel bad leaving you behind, she'd said while they sat together in the sauna at their gym.

You're not leaving me behind, you're living your own life, Tess said, only half believing it.

But maybe the truth needed to be said again. "I don't want to be in Atlanta doing the same things every weekend and wondering what other experiences I could be having," Tess murmured, feeling like the words were being dug out of her her. "But I'm too scared to do anything about it. And now you're going off on your big adventure and leaving me behind."

"Honey, no. It's not like that."

"Oh my God, you two are really bringing me down here." Lisa knocked back her glass of mimosa with a huff and signaled the waiter for another one. She looked exasperated. "I know I tend to oversimplify things, but why don't you just leave? Move to the same town as Maya and be done with it?"

"My family——" Tess began but Lisa cut her off.

"Your sister is a leech. The others couldn't care less if you disappeared from the planet."

The brutality of it took Tess' breath away. She shoved back from the table. "You're out of line, Lisa."

"But am I lying?"

"I think…" Tess drew a deep enough breath to help relieve the ache in her chest. It felt especially painful since she'd just talked to Tracy. "I think it's time for me to go."

"No!" Maya grabbed for her hand but Tess pulled away.

"It's okay. I'll just see you tomorrow, okay?"

"No, that's not okay." She lashed Lisa with one of her fiercest glares and jumped up from her chair.

Lisa glanced at Tess like she didn't know what the hell she just did. At the same time Tam said, "You can be such an out-of-pocket bitch, Lisa."

Making a sound of frustration, Maya pulled Tess away from the table and through the carpeted and quiet dining room, out toward the front of the hotel. Valeted cars passed steadily past them.

"Don't listen to anything Lisa says, honey."

"It's not like she's lying though, right?" Tess crossed her arms under her breasts ignoring her best friend's silent plea to look at her.

"We all know it's not that simple."

"Do we?"

"Yes, we do. You have your sister, the job you've had for years, your whole life here in Atlanta. Of course, you can't just pack a suitcase and leave." Even Maya didn't sound convinced of her own words anymore, not after almost twenty years of repeating them whenever Tess convinced her to stay in the city they'd long outgrown.

It couldn't go on like this.

"I love you, Maya." Tess smiled tenderly at her friend, loving her now more than ever. "I'm all right, really. I just let Lisa's judgmental bullshit get to me. This week is about you, nothing else. Your wedding day is in two days. That's all that matters."

Maya looked relieved, then guilty for being relieved. Tess pulled her into a hug. "Come on. Let's go finish the rest of those mimosas and get you ready for one of the biggest days of your life."

The wedding, when it came, was a beautiful blur. Tess remembered crying as she stood by her best friend's side and Maya officially linked her life with someone else. Tess ate cake with the bridesmaids, danced, laughed, blew kisses to Maya as she was being swept up into her new husband's arms and into the honeymoon suite at the hotel housing them all for the night. Pink rose blossoms everywhere, and echoes of the conversation they'd had over mimosas haunting her.

Then it was over.

She stood at the edge of the lake with her hands in the pockets of her maid of honor dress, the tulle swaying around her legs in the breeze, the smell of sun-warmed roses in the air. The rain that had threatened all day began to fall and the cool raindrops slid over her bare shoulders, down her arms.

Briefly, she had a moment's thought about her hair. Then dismissed it. The wedding was over. There was no one left to impress.

Truly, she had nothing left in Atlanta. Nothing. She turned her face up to the rain, memories falling all around her—Elijah, Maya, her sister, Elijah again. She drew in a deep breath and tasted the familiar flavor of fear on her tongue.

She was tired of it.

In the week since Lisa had confronted her about Elijah, Tess saw him four times, each time was more intoxicating than the last and each time he left her bed, she found it harder and harder to let him go. They'd shared pillows, secrets, concerns for the future in a way two people in their position had no business doing. But it felt exhilarating. Fearless.

And now, Elijah's bags were packed and ready for wherever it was he was off to next. Like Maya, he was leaving her, too.

Tess' stomach dipped and she turned in an angry swirl of tulle to head back to the hotel. Her flats pressed into the muddying bank of the lakeside with a sound like wet kisses as she pushed through the raindrops slapping against her skin. Lightning slashed across the sky illuminating the outline of the colonial style hotel.

Alone, she rushed up the flower-lined walkway toward the elegant sprawl of the hotel, most people sensible enough to have gone inside and left the rain to fools like her. The lightning flashed again and showed the glowing shape of a man walking into the rain. Toward the lake, toward her.

Tess stopped and breath fled her parted lips.

"The wedding was nice," she said when she could speak. "You'd have liked it."

Elijah walked toward her, slow and ambling as if the rain and lightning meant nothing to him. And maybe it didn't. "Did it break your heart?" They'd talked of shared heartbreaks before.

The pressed her teeth into her lower lip, put her hands back in her pockets. "Not as much as I thought it would," she said.

"I'm glad."

"Me too."

They stood in the rain together and lightning flashed again followed too quickly by a crash of thunder that made Tess jump. But she didn't run for shelter.

"When are you leaving?" She asked the question that had been on her mind since he told her he was moving out of Atlanta.

"Not until after graduation. Another two months."

Tess looked up at the sky and rain fell into her eyes. Everything blurred. "You feel like company?"

"That's why I came." He mirrored her, hands in the pockets of his jeans, watching.

She curled and uncurled her fingers in her pockets, calculating the risks of allowing him to misunderstand her. Then she took the leap. "I don't mean here. I mean…" She made a gesture to encompass the world, everything beyond Atlanta.

He didn't look surprised. "That's why I came," he said again. This time, a smile captured the shape of his mouth and showed her the flash of his bright teeth against cedar skin. "In the spirit of new beginnings," Elijah tipped his head toward the remnants of the wedding decorations getting wet in the rain. The yellow gauze strung between the trees, the paper lanterns, the army of cloth-draped chairs. "Come to London with me."

"Oh!" The name of the city on his lips zinged excitement down Tess's spine. Just like it had the first time he said it all those nights ago while they lay in her bed. She smiled, the unease and uncertainty melting away with each new drop of rain on her skin. "Okay." Tess pressed her lips together around her smile. "I'm ready to go whenever you are."

Predictably, he grinned and came closer, happiness like fireflies in the warm glow of his eyes. "It'll be a couple of months," he reminded her.

"Plenty of time to get ready," Tess said.

Then she took Elijah's hand, and allowed him to lead her out of the rain.

Thank you!

Thank you so much for reading **Seducing the Stripper**! If you enjoyed it, please take the time to write a starred review online – it doesn't have to be a long one – and share your experience with a friend or three.

To find me on the interwebs, go to my website www. LindsayEvansWrites.com, my Facebook, or Twitter pages. You can even use old-fashioned email at Lindsay EvansXOX@gmail.com.

Excerpt - A Delicate Affair

Golden knew he was in trouble when she walked in.

Brown skin, thick hair, a lioness of a woman striding with a pride of other beauties wearing expensive dresses. They were obviously rich. Young. At least, younger than the crowd that usually ended up at Rosie's juke joint. Younger than Golden's twenty-six. More than half the men in the crowded, smoky dance bar turned to watch the three of them, but he only saw her.

Clive, a guy Golden trusted and who was the reason he had the luck of playing at Rosie's in the first place, jerked his head up from the piano and tilted his head at Golden. The sign for, "What's going on?"

Damn. Ten years, on-and-off, of being friends with Golden apparently gave Clive a clue when Golden's attention veered away from where it should have been.

Golden tipped his head toward the door. Clive, not missing a single key on the piano he played like a madman, looked over at the girls. No way would his friend know which one had made Golden just about swallow his tongue.

"No chance." His friend merely mouthed the words, rolled his eyes, and gave his full attention to the ragtime he pounded out of the piano, placed sideways so Clive could see the audience and rile them up when he stood, shaking out one long leg and then the other, dancing while he played. The music-hungry Saturday night crowd ate it up.

In front of the stage, the sunken dance floor was packed body-to-body. People danced and gyrated and generally had a good-old time while the music played. Marley, the only woman in their band of four, belted out songs about heartbreak and lust while Winston, quiet and quietly intense, tormented the crowd with a rhythm from his pair of tall African drums.

Even though the place was crammed packed to the rafters, Big Ed, the galoot by the front door, hustled over to take care of the giggling girls. He waved them toward a table near the front of the stage and off the side from the dancers. Damn near within touching distance, if Golden got bold enough. He plucked at the strings of his banjo, improvising around Clive's loud and lively rag.

Golden's fingers were sore from playing all night, but he was having too much fun to care. The crowd was jumping and that girl was hot as the fire in his mama's kitchen.

Watching her, he didn't so much as twitch the wrong way. He couldn't mess up the music. Only he—and Clive—knew he was sweating like a hog at the butcher with that fine girl breezing between tables to sit at the big one up front.

Golden knew Rosie, the owner of the juke joint and a notoriously ornery woman, had been saving the main table for her man. But as soon as the girls gestured toward the table with their perfumed and pampered fingers, Rosie gave it up easier than a whore on Saturday night. Those rich girls meant money in her pocket.

Golden had only been in Washington, D.C. for about seven months, but he had already seen what money and power could buy. The only difference up here was that the money and influence was thrown around by Negroes, and people jumped up mighty quick to do whatever these rich Negroes wanted.

The band's latest song wound down to almost nothing and, suddenly, Golden felt everything he'd been too lost in the music to notice before. The sweat running down his face. The rough chafing of the new suit at his wrists every time he moved his hands along the banjo. The hunger that cramped his belly from not eating since his morning shift at Joe's, the restaurant where he worked most days.

Anyone not dancing clapped and jumped to their feet while the rich girls spread themselves around the table, chattering with each other and looking around like they were at a zoo or something. With their bright clothes and brighter laughter, they were like the gems scattered in his mama's jewelry box.

One girl wore red, another green. But the one he couldn't keep his eyes off wore white. Bits of the dress sparkled, and she seemed like a diamond among the others. Expensive and untouchable, cool despite her loud and frequent laughter.

From the way they leaned toward Big Ed and stopped him from walking off, Golden could tell they were demanding drinks. But Big Ed shook his head and gestured back toward the kitchen, where the waitresses were tending to the other customers' drink and food orders. After another emphatic shake of Big Ed's massive noggin, the girls seemed to simmer down. Ed shuffled away as fast as his big body could carry him.

"More! More! More!" The crowd chanted and stomped their feet the way they did every night when the music stopped even for a minute.

The girls settled down and, with a few ringing notes on the piano keys, Clive started up another number. Golden wiped his forehead with the already damp rag he carried in his pocket, stretched his fingers, then poured himself back into the music.

For the length of another set, he managed to forget about the diamond girl and her glittering friends. But at the end of the set, the band scattered. Clive went off to find his girl lurking at the back of the bar, watching for any other woman ready to grab her man. Winston ran to the john to sniff whatever foolishness he had up his nose. Marley, who dressed every day in suits and ties, dipped out the back alley door to grab a smoke. Golden followed.

Instead of standing outside Rosie's back door like the customers did, Golden walked a few yards away to the awning of Swiss Jewel Emporium. The Emporium had been closed nearly a month now. In this neighborhood, it was tough for a high-class place like that, specializing in expensive watches and gems, to survive. Too bad, since Golden had liked the owners, two guys from someplace in Europe. They didn't chase him off when he came in nearly every day to gawk at the cases filled with glittering rings and necklaces. Those pretty things reminded him of his mother and her love of all things shiny.

Golden settled under the Emporium's awning with his back to the rough brick wall and a cigarette in his hand. He stiffened at the sound of footsteps and only relaxed when Marley made herself comfortable just a couple of feet away. He didn't tell her to kick off. As social as she could be, Marley had her own reasons for keeping away from the crowd gathered at Rosie's back door.

Golden was fresh to the city and still trying to get the hang of this smoking thing. Damn near everybody, including Clive, who he'd known back in Opal, said that real city men smoked. Golden didn't see the sense in it, but he had to admit it gave him the excuse to step away from the crowd and sit in his own quiet for a while. He still wasn't used to the rush and noise of the city, of people everywhere and the near-constant clang and clatter of his too-close neighbors. Sometimes, it was just too much. Although he was pushed out of Opal at the threat of a noose for looking at a white girl—which was bull because he preferred his girls as black as his coffee—Golden missed home.

He still longed for those quiet Southern evenings, nights of glow bugs and cicadas and the full moon burning a clear path across a field of peach trees. Seven months and he still yearned for all those things like crazy. But he wasn't returning to Georgia. He had a plan, and it didn't include moving backward.

"I'm heading to the john." Marley tossed her cigarette butt into a nearby puddle. Just before they'd got to the club that night, the rain had come and gone in a flash and left the streets wet but the skies clear.

"All right," Golden said, rolling his still-unlit cig between two fingers. "See you inside."

After Marley took off, Golden tucked the cig into the corner of his mouth and leaned into the bumpy bricks at his back. He loosened his muscles one at a time and breathed out around the cigarette, long and deep.

These days, it seemed to take a lot of work for him to relax.

He'd only just closed his eyes when the sound of raindrops drew him back to the present and into the musty alley. He looked up. From under the protection of the awning, the rain was almost nice. If the idea of walking back to his place in the rain and mud didn't threaten to ruin his one good pair of suit pants, he'd like it more.

Still, it was hard to be mad when a piece of the South visited him in the city like this. Light raindrops falling from the sky, lit by the streetlamps, aglow and surreal.

"That's not how you smoke a cigarette, you know."

The alley wasn't dark, but it was long, just a narrow strip between the building that housed Rosie's and the Emporium on one side and a combination liquor/department store on the other.

A woman walked toward Golden. It seemed like she materialized out of the air. She wore white and floated through the sprinkles of rain with an unlit smoke of her own held between long fingers. The diamond girl.

Golden almost swallowed his cigarette. It was only when he was fumbling to keep it from going down his throat that he heard a flurry of giggling conversation near Rosie's. What the hell? Two other girls stood between him and Rosie's door. They didn't look like they belonged anywhere near an alley. They watched him and Diamond Girl.

She came closer.

"Light me up?" Diamond Girl held the cig under her chin, protecting it from the raindrops sprinkling over her hair and pretty white dress.

The chain from a watch glinted gold against the dress and disappeared into a small pocket at her waist. The sight of her away from the noise and crowd punched him in the chest.

God damn, she was pretty.

Fighting breathlessness, Golden fumbled in his pocket for the silver match safe he hadn't yet pulled out for himself. He lit one of the matches with a flick of his fingernail and lifted the flame to the cig already at the girl's dark red lips. She sucked on the white stem of the cig. The tip flared red. In the combined glow from the lit cigarette and the street lamps, her skin looked danger-ously soft.

Damn. Just…damn.

No way a woman should be that good looking and not be in a magazine, or a museum.

A smile blossomed on her face, like she knew what he was thinking. Blowing a plume of smoke to the side, she took the glowing cig from her mouth. "That's how you smoke, baby," she said.

He took the one out of his mouth, held it between two fingers, and looked down at it like it had done him some wrong. "It's not really my thing, anyway," he said. "Cigarettes make my mouth taste like ashes."

"Like ashes?" With the burning cig in one hand, elbow bent and balanced in the palm of her other hand, she quirked her moist lips. "What about my mouth, would it taste like ashes, too?"

Shock and a sudden blast of desire shot up Golden's

spine. But while his brain was wrecked at the very thought of sipping from her rosy lips, his mouth opened up to save him. "Probably, and it's not a flavor I'm fond of," he said. "No matter where it's coming from."

The quality of the woman's smile changed, becoming less flirty and more flinty, like she'd taken his rejection to taste the cigarette from her mouth personally.

"You're not from around here, are you?" Just like before, she didn't wait for his response. She raised her voice. "Sounds like you just fell off a peach truck fresh from down South."

His fingers tightened around the unlit cigarette. Did this woman just…?

A rush of heat, part humiliation but mostly anger, scorched him from head to toe. Golden knew if they'd been in the bright sun, she would have been able to see every shade of furious red rushing under his pale yellow skin.

Giggles from her friends scurried at him like small spiders.

Golden shoved the match safe in his pocket hard enough to feel a seam break. "I come from somewhere it's considered uncouth and low class to be rude." He looked down at her from his height of just over six feet and realized, even in the midst of his anger, she was only a few inches shorter than he was, the perfect height for kissing.

Snarling at himself, he tucked the limp cigarette behind his ear and stalked toward the entrance of Rosie's, ignoring the pair of brightly dressed girls who gawked at him and giggled some more.

"Did you lose your catch, Leonie?" A woman's

teasing voice rolled down the alley and followed him into the dance hall. One of Diamond Girl's friends.

Golden had always been a laid-back guy and never liked it when folks flew off the handle because somebody said something they didn't like. But, damn it if he didn't understand why they got so mad. Nothing made him more ornery than somebody treating him like an idiot just because he was from down South. Especially other Negroes.

Inside Rosie's, he waded through the press of hot bodies and the smell of booze to hop back on the stage.

"What's the word with the hot piece that followed you out to the alley?" Clive closed his fancy cigarette case and put a smoke between his lips. Like most people, he smoked inside the club. He didn't need the same escape Golden did. "She looked hot for you, that's for sure."

"Nobody followed me anywhere. The girl was just getting some air with her friends."

"Didn't look like it to me."

"Seems like you better get your eyes checked then." He tried to make a joke of it with a slap to Clive's skinny shoulder.

Winston and Marley had already returned to the stage and were settling in. Marley tossed back her last swallow of liquor and slid the glass over the floor, out of everybody's way. At the front of the stage, she cleared her throat, getting ready.

"Let's make this money so I can go home with my girl," Winston said.

He wasn't the only one hoping to catch the slippery fish of success at the end of the line. Golden had his eye on bigger things, too. His dreams didn't end here in the nation's capital, where the colored help could play music all night long on stage but weren't allowed to sit at a table and enjoy the show with everyone else. Those whites-only places bothered him more than all the others. Here, Negroes like him were good enough to entertain but not human enough to deserve their own entertainment.

"Yeah," Clive said with a snicker. "And maybe Golden boy, here, can get that girl out there who's been eyeing him all night."

Golden snorted and grabbed his banjo. He played a few bars to warm up his fingers and then dove into the sweet shelter of his music. In front, the jewel girls sat at their fancy table, obviously eyeing him, but he managed to ignore them for the rest of the night.

In bed, much later that night, it was another story.

Diamond Girl found him in his dreams.

There, she was an ebony goddess with fire-red lips who hovered over him and teased him with her body. When she kissed him, she left the taste of ashes on his tongue. Golden woke up twisted in his sheets, his chest and belly heaving and damp with sweat from the lustful labor of his dreams. He burned.

His entire body was a hard and hungry ache not even the crude touch of his own hand could satisfy. A short while later, with the slick of his release drying on his hand and belly, he panted roughly at the ceiling.

If he never saw that girl again, it would be too soon.

A Delicate Affair, Available now.

Also by Lindsay Evans

A Delicate Affair (historical novella)

Affair of Pleasure

Bare Pleasures

CEO's Dilemma (with Kayla Perrin)

Dim the Lights (novella)

Her Perfect Pleasure

On-Air Passion

Pleasure Under the Sun

Seducing the Stripper

Snowy Mountain Nights

Sultry Pleasure

The Pleasure of His Company

The Wrong Fiancé (with Niobia Bryant)

To Tempt a Husband

Untamed Love

About the Author

Jamaican-born Lindsay Evans currently lives and writes in Atlanta, GA. A writer of sensual love stories and decadent erotica, she loves good food and romance and would happily travel to the ends of the earth for both. Her novel, To Tempt a Husband, is now available. Find out more at LindsayEvansWrites.com.